"Why don't you l

Keaton appeared taken aback. "I never said I didn't like you. I just...don't have time for women like you."

"'Like me,' how?"

"You wear designer clothes. You drive a fancy import. You talk a mile a minute and listen with less patience than a two-year-old."

"Anything else?"

"Isn't that enough?"

"More than enough." Pointing at him with her teaspoon, she said, "I guess all the women you date are far different."

A muscle in his cheek twitched. "I don't date."

"Maybe you should." Tessa was fully aware that her tone had become snippy. "Maybe you should get your own life so you can stop judging mine."

Dear Reader,

The inspiration for *Simple Gifts* is a personal one. Years ago, I taught a very special boy. He was bright, inquisitive and hardworking.

He was also homeless.

I worried about him. We became close. Then, one day... he was gone. I never heard from him again, never knew what happened to him. All I knew for certain was that I wished I could have helped him more than I did.

When my heroine, Tessa McGuiry, meets Wes in an alley behind the boutique she manages, she knows her life is about to change. When she asks her neighbor Keaton Phillips for help with the boy, she finds out love can bloom between even the most dissimilar people.

I hope you enjoy this story. People ask all the time who I base my characters on. Truthfully, I make them up! However, one thing always shines through.... I like to write stories about good people I would like to know In the case of Tessa, Keaton and Wes, that couldn't be more true.

If you have a moment, write to me and tell me what you thought, at www.shelleygalloway.com. I love to hea from readers. And...happy Thanksgiving! Here's hoping you'll have a day filled with family and friends...and time to give thanks for all the "simple" things in life.

Shelley Galloway

SIMPLE GIFTS

Shelley Galloway

TORONTO • NEW YORK • LONDON
AMSTERDAM • PARIS • SYDNEY • HAMBURG
STOCKHOLM • ATHENS • TOKYO • MILAN • MADRID
PRAGUE • WARSAW • BUDAPEST • AUCKLAND

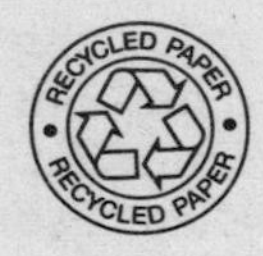

ISBN-13: 978-0-373-75138-9
ISBN-10: 0-373-75138-9

SIMPLE GIFTS

This edition published by arrangement with Harlequin Books S.A.

www.eHarlequin.com

Printed in U.S.A.

ABOUT THE AUTHOR

Shelley Galloway loves to get up early, drink too much coffee and write books. These pastimes come in handy during her day-to-day life in southern Ohio. Most days she can be found driving her kids to their activities, writing romances in her basement or trying to find a way to get ahead of her pile of laundry. She's also been known to bug her husband to talk to her, since she spends an inordinate amount of time alone.

Shelley taught school for over a decade before turning to her first love of writing. She was thrilled to find out that *Cinderella Christmas,* her first novel with Harlequin, made the Waldenbooks bestseller list. Shelley also happens to spend a lot of time online. Please visit her Web site at www.shelleygalloway.com.

Books by Shelley Galloway

HARLEQUIN AMERICAN ROMANCE

1090—CINDERELLA CHRISTMAS

To Heather, Cathy, Hilda and Julie.
My writing buddies!
Tuesdays would never be the same without you.

And, of course, to Tom.
It takes a special man to hand-sell
romance novels during business trips.

Chapter One

"Tessa, while I realize sorting scarves has a certain *je ne sais quoi*, time is of the essence. We have appointments scheduled all afternoon. Did you unpack the shipment from Hermès yet?"

Tessa McGuiry winced at her boss's butchered pronunciation of the French expression. Though Sylvia kept her Cincinnati boutique stocked with all the latest designer accessories from Europe and beyond, she certainly had no talent when it came to foreign languages.

"The Hermès bags are on the shelves," Tessa said. "I also inventoried the Michael Kors belts and took three orders from customers." She hated when Sylvia made it seem as though she'd been slacking. She was the hardest worker there.

"Oh. Well, it's the fall rush, darlin'. Just be sure you keep up." Sylvia snapped her fingers for emphasis.

Repressing a groan, Tessa nodded. "I'll do my

best," she said, thinking to herself what an unlikely pair they made. Sylvia owned S.Y.D., Sylvia York Designs, but Tessa managed it. Sylvia flitted through the high-end boutique on spiky heels, while Tessa strove to make the place run like clockwork.

Sylvia was given awards and accolades for her boutique and her original designs—some of which she'd asked for Tessa's input on. Meanwhile, Tessa was given silly to-do lists for things she'd already done.

"I thought I'd work on the window display," Tessa said. "The samples for our spring line just came in."

Sylvia shrugged. "You know I don't have time to do it myself. But check on the new shipment from FedEx first, then set up a display for our cashmere accessories. If we don't push them, we're going to have three boxes of gloves and scarves in the back room."

She'd already done that, too. *Of course she had.* Sylvia was standing right in front of the display. Didn't she notice *anything?*

Sometimes Tessa felt as though S.Y.D. meant more to her than it did to Sylvia. It was going to be hard to leave here eventually, but someday… Someday she hoped her reputation at S.Y.D. would propel her to a better job—and her dream of owning a boutique and selling her own designs.

But there was no reason to tell Sylvia any of that. "All right."

"And call Mrs. Hockmann and offer our services,"

Sylvia added, looking up from her BlackBerry. "She's getting married. Again."

Sylvia York Designs had helped with Mrs. Hockmann's last two weddings. "Will do," Tessa said, biting her lip in order to hold her tongue. "I'll call her as soon as I finish sorting these scarves."

But her promise fell on deaf ears. Sylvia had already opened the front door. "Bye!" She waved and Tessa waved back. Gladly.

Sylvia tended to waltz in and out of the shop as if she didn't have a care in the world—she was lucky that Tessa cared enough for both of them.

As the antique door closed with a dignified whoosh, Tessa threw her head back in frustration. Would Sylvia ever acknowledge all the things she did for her? Was it too much to ask for a little recognition?

"Is the coast clear?" Jillian asked, emerging from one of the velvet-curtained dressing rooms with a bemused smile.

Tessa arched an eyebrow in her direction. "Just barely. You know, you could've come out and given me some support."

"I probably could have, but I decided against it. *You're* the manager. *I'm* only a lowly employee."

Tessa was pretty sure Jillian Lane had never been an only anything. When she'd come to S.Y.D., she'd infused the place with a much-needed burst of energy. In many ways, Jillian was the exact opposite of Tessa. She went to church regularly, had a steady boyfriend and even owned a dog. In short, Jillian had a relatively normal, stable life whereas Tessa was still trying to figure out what to do with hers. Yet, as different as they were, the two of them had become fast friends. "Tell me again why you're working here."

Jillian frowned. "The great pay and benefits?"

Tessa laughed at the obvious joke and added, "Don't forget the discount."

"I'd never forget the discount. It really *is* good."

Pointing to the piece of paper Sylvia had handed her, Tessa said, "We've just been given a to-do list about a mile long."

"Sylvia actually came up with things we haven't done yet?"

"Believe it or not, she did."

Jillian grabbed the sheet and whistled. "This should only take us a couple of hours. I can't wait until the day I work for somebody else. I hear people love her former employees."

"That's because when we get regular hours and real pay we're grateful."

She, Jillian and Ryan—their other coworker—were constantly on their feet, designing window displays, dressing mannequins and helping demanding customers. Tessa felt the burden of being in charge without having complete authority. If she wasn't so afraid of failing, she would've started her own shop a long time ago.

Tessa glanced at the list again. "I'll go call Mrs.

Hockmann. Will you clean up and begin unboxing the jewelry from Neveux?" As Tessa took in all the work that needed to be done, she asked, "Where is Ryan, anyway?"

"At night school."

"Oh, right." Ryan was finishing up a degree in business and fashion merchandising, clearly hoping to be the manager at S.Y.D. one day. It was yet another reason to think about opening her own boutique soon.

For the next few hours, Tessa and Jillian were kept busy with customers. Each person who walked through the door was treated to the boutique's trademark service.

But today, Tessa was really struggling with how much longer she could put on such a façade. Everything in S.Y.D. was too extravagant, too expensive, too…everything.

She knew her parents would be appalled at her daily priorities. Her father was a doctor, and her mother was actively involved in several charities. They'd raised her to remember that there was more to a person than her looks, more to life than money and material things. In fact, she purposely hadn't shared many details of her job with them because she knew they'd wonder how she could feel fulfilled helping rich ladies look good.

And every so often, especially when she had a bad day, Tessa would wonder the same thing.

The front door chimed again, and in strode Mrs.

Edwards, a charming older woman with a penchant for faux-fur-lined accessories. "You have anything new, Tessa, dear?"

"As a matter of fact, we do." Part of the reason everyone liked S.Y.D. was that there was always something new. "If you'll have a seat, I'll bring over some silk scarves we just got in from Italy."

"I'd like tea, too. With lemon. No cream," she said, perching on one of the citron-colored chairs near a glass étagère.

"Yes, ma'am."

"And a cookie. Shortbread, if you have it."

"Tea and a cookie. I'll be right back," Tessa said over her shoulder, as she headed toward the rear of the store.

"Maybe you could perform circus tricks, too," Jillian whispered to Tessa when she walked into the back room. "Or vacuum her car."

Tessa wouldn't put it past any of her customers to demand anything. "At least Mrs. Edwards is pleasant," she said. "And she does always appreciate everything we do for her."

"Plus she's a fan of yours, Tessa. I've overheard her singing your praises to other customers."

"That's good to hear." Tessa genuinely liked working with the customers. She enjoyed helping them with their outfits, especially when they were shopping for a special occasion. Sometimes, she just wished her job had more purpose.

"Oh, Tessa, I'd like to try on one of the new suits,

too," Mrs. Edwards called out. Tessa peered into the showroom to see the older woman motioning toward a mannequin modeling a thousand-dollar wool outfit that Tessa had helped Sylvia design. The request brought her a feeling of satisfaction.

"Absolutely. I'll be there in a second," she answered, quickly pouring hot water into a china cup. "Could you find some cookies?" she asked Jillian, before gracefully walking back into the salon.

An hour later, Tessa felt as if she was about to collapse. Mrs. Edwards had left, but not before ordering a suit and buying several hundred dollars' worth of silk scarves.

"The time is 9:05," Jillian announced, mimicking the automated voice in the Cincinnati airport trains. "Our front door is now closing."

As Jillian clicked the bolt in place, Tessa clapped. "We made it through another day."

"Yep. Now we've just got to get this place ready for tomorrow's fashion show."

"Let me go out back and toss these empty boxes in the recycling," Tessa said. "There are so many, we can hardly move in the storage area."

"Good luck, it's freezing out there."

After flattening four boxes, Tessa opened the back door and was assaulted by a blast of frigid air. "Well, tomorrow *is* the beginning of October," she muttered to herself as she propped open the door and made her way to the Dumpster.

The alley behind the strip mall was cramped and poorly lit. Large brown Dumpsters lined the south side, casting ominous shadows. Being in the alley always made her a bit nervous. Especially in the evening. Especially in the rain.

Seeking to calm her nerves, she resorted to her favorite activity, imagining all the junk food she'd have when she got home. "Tonight I'm going to take a hot bath and put my feet up," she said out loud. "Then I'm going to eat pizza, and maybe even an entire carton of chocolate chip ice cream for dessert."

She shifted the bulky cardboard under her arm, teetering on her high heels as she did so. "And I'm going to put on old sweats. And slippers. Cozy ones."

Her breath made little white clouds in the air. "*Then* I'm going to sleep for six whole hours," she finished, to no one but herself.

Except she wasn't alone.

There was a scurry of motion, and she noticed a faint shadow in the distance. Her heart began to palpitate. "Hello?" she asked, shielding her body with the four boxes.

No answer. Just shuffling.

Something clinked to the ground.

Tessa inhaled sharply, coughing as cold air raced through her lungs. There really was someone out there, but that person was a lot smaller than she'd first thought. In fact, the shadow seemed to be about half her size.

Almost childlike.

Concern reverberated through her at the thought. No child should be anywhere near a vacant alley.

Raising her voice, she called out, "Hello?"

Still no answer, although the shadow moved slightly closer.

Summoning her courage, Tessa stepped closer, as well. Now she was definitely curious. The puddles on the ground were beginning to turn to ice. No one who could be anywhere else would be outside tonight. "Is anyone here?" she asked again.

More silence.

Tessa's body tensed. She was painfully aware that she was being watched by a stranger. Just as she raised her arms to hurl the boxes in the Dumpster, the shadow shifted. In the dim light flowing from the open doorway, a small face appeared.

A boy's. He probably wasn't more than ten or eleven years old. He had dirty blond hair and was staring at her with scared-looking eyes.

What was he doing in the alley?

Quickly, Tessa got rid of the boxes and walked over to him.

His eyes widened as she approached, but he didn't say anything, only breathed hard.

"What are you doing out here?" Tessa asked gently. "Did you need something?"

"No."

"No? Are you sure?"

He lowered his head before mumbling, "Cans."

She had no idea what he was talking about. "Cans? Are you thirsty?"

As if surprised that she could be so dense, he said, "No. I'm looking for old cans. For cash."

"At night?"

"Yeah," he muttered, seeming to favor one-word explanations.

"Oh." She glanced behind him down the alley. "Where are your parents?"

"My mom's down the street."

Tessa craned her neck but didn't see anyone. "She shouldn't let you be doing this by yourself. You should be home, in bed. It's freezing out."

Again, he looked at her as if she was a complete idiot. "We live in our car. The car needs gas."

Hence, the cans, she thought to herself. *You are an idiot.* "My name is Tessa. What's yours?"

"Wes."

"How old are you?"

His shoulders stiffened. "Ten."

She studied him closely. He wore an old jacket that looked about three sizes too big, too-short jeans and old tennis shoes. No gloves. "Wes, hold on."

She ran into the shop's backroom and grabbed two bags of cookies, then dug inside her desk drawer and pulled out her cashmere-blend black gloves. When she returned, she thrust both toward him. "Here. Have you had anything to eat lately?"

Wes looked at her offering, then at his hands. They

were clutching a black half-empty trash bag. "No, thanks," he said.

There was no way she could just leave him. "Please take the gloves, at the very least. They'll keep your hands warm."

"Nah."

She thought quickly. "For your mom?"

A glimmer of hope appeared on his face. Without a word, he dropped the sack, took the gloves and put them in his coat pockets.

Tessa heard a faint call from the far end of the alley. Wes's eyes widened and he picked up his bag. "That's my mom. She's sick. I gotta go."

"Wait. Here," she said, stuffing the bags of cookies under one of his arms. "Take these back to your mom." *Didn't she still have a twenty in her wallet?* "Hey, if you hold on for one more second, I'll give you some money. You know, for gas?"

He lifted his chin. "We don't need your money."

"Oh. Sure." Realizing she'd embarrassed him, but unwilling to let him go, she racked her brain for a way to see him again. "You know, I have a bunch of cans at home. A lot. Come back tomorrow night and I'll give them to you."

He looked skeptical. "Crushed?"

She could do that. "Yes."

"There's a lot?"

"Oh, yeah," she said without hesitation. "At least a hundred."

"Okay."

She exhaled, feeling as if she'd accomplished a great feat. "Good." They stared at each other as Wes's mom called him again.

The boy stepped back. "I've got to go."

Knowing she was prying, she whispered, "You going to be okay tonight?"

After a second's pause, he shrugged. "Sure."

His optimism was hard to swallow.

As if sensing her skepticism, his wan face broke into a fragile grin. "My mom says things always work out sooner or later. Tonight I got new gloves and a bunch of cookies, right?"

Taken aback, she could only nod. "See you tomorrow?"

"I'll try. Bye," he said, before disappearing into the night.

A big gust of wind blew through the alley, bringing with it a taste of snow. Tessa closed her eyes as the tiny particles stung her cheeks. Suddenly the alley didn't feel quite as scary anymore. After one short conversation, it had become a meeting place—a place to look forward to returning in twenty-four hours.

She thought about Wes, the gloves and his mother's words. *Did* things usually work out, sooner or later? The wind whipped through her hair as Tessa gazed toward the other end of the alley, wondering what Wes was doing now.

Had he given his mom the gloves? Were they eating her cookies? Would they ever come back?

What would she do if they didn't?

Her own mother's favorite saying raced through her mind: *Everything happens for a reason.*

Was tonight's meeting one of those meant-to-be things? After all, it wasn't often that she took boxes to the Dumpster at night.

"Tessa?" Jillian called out, interrupting her musings. "What are you doing? You're going to freeze."

In a daze, Tessa turned to her friend. "What?"

"Come inside!"

Obediently, she followed her and felt the warm air begin to thaw her frozen cheeks as soon as she closed the door.

Jillian eyed Tessa with concern. "You okay?"

"I don't know. There was a boy out there."

Jillian's brow furrowed. "What?"

"A boy. Ten years old. He was collecting cans. I gave him the cookies. He's…homeless."

Jillian opened the door again, obviously ready to help.

"He's gone now," Tessa said, stopping her friend. "He went back to where his mother was waiting in a car."

"The poor thing."

"He looked as if he needed a friend."

"I bet he did." Staring at the door, Jillian frowned. "It's dangerous to be alone in an alley with a stranger, though. You should've called me. Remember the story on the news a couple of nights ago? The one about the woman who was attacked in her back alley? You can't be too careful."

"I know. But I've got to tell you, I felt something for this boy." She snapped her fingers. "Cans. We need empty crushed cans. Wes was collecting them. Do you think you could bring me at least twenty by tomorrow? I'll ask Ryan to do the same."

"Wouldn't it be better to have some food or clothing for him?"

Remembering how he'd refused her money, Tessa shook her head. "I don't think he'd accept it. Promise me you'll bring some cans."

"I promise."

"Thanks." Tessa turned on the vacuum, not eager to answer any more questions. Or to hear how Jillian might have handled everything so much better. She innately did everything better.

Tessa wasn't the jealous type, but at the moment, she couldn't help feeling a bit green-eyed. She was sure if Jillian had been the one to find Wes, she would've met his mom, given him some money and made sure he'd be all right. She seemed to instinctively know how to deal with situations like these.

Tessa had only a determined will.

On the drive home, Tessa couldn't stop thinking about Wes. She was worried about him. He'd looked so little and worn out.

He needed more than some silly cans for gas money. He needed real help from someone whose job it was to solve these types of problems.

And unfortunately, she knew exactly whom she should talk to: Keaton Phillips, her neighbor. He lived in the apartment above her. He was sullen, terse and didn't much care for her, especially since she'd complained to him about his workout schedule. He liked to work out at ungodly hours of the morning, which meant she'd hear the clunk-clunk of his free weights hitting the floor right above her head at 5:00 a.m. When she'd dared suggest that he wait until daylight, he hadn't taken it well.

She attributed his unwillingness to cooperate to the fact that she'd offended him early on, when they'd first crossed paths. She'd tried on several occasions to engage him in conversation, but he'd only answered in monosyllables or grunts—leading her to accuse him of being antisocial.

He'd never been to a single function in their complex. Just a few weeks before the weight-lifting incident, he'd glared at her when she'd walked by him on her way to the complex's end-of-summer softball game, and commented that she had too much spare time on her hands.

No, things between them weren't great. They were barely tolerable. But...he was a cop. And their landlady thought he was pretty terrific.

He'd been cited in the paper, not only for his work

on the force, but also for volunteering in the community. She'd read that he regularly helped serve meals at homeless shelters and tutored kids at a charter school downtown.

So, while he'd probably never give *her* the time of day, she knew without a doubt that Keaton Phillips would know how to help Wes.

Some things mattered so much more than frustrations at work or petty disagreements.

Funny how she'd just started to remember that.

Chapter Two

"I'm really sorry to bother you, but I need your help," Tessa blurted as soon as Keaton opened the door.

Bleary-eyed, and feeling more than a little tired, he blinked hard. Why was his flighty neighbor standing in his doorway? Over the past year, he'd done his best to avoid Tessa McGuiry. So much about her irked him. The way she'd complained about his workout schedule. The way she acted as if their complex was a sorority house instead of just a place to live.

The way she'd continually tried to be his friend, before she'd given up. She now cast sullen looks at him whenever they passed each other in the parking lot.

"Keaton!" she practically yelled. As if she was his mother or something. But there was an edge to her voice. A desperation.

He studied her again, this time more critically. No apparent injuries, no blood or bruises marring her too-pretty face. Her blue eyes looked as clear and bright as always. Her light-brown hair was fussily styled, as usual, and her clothes appeared neat as ever. Three-inch heels peeked out from under a thick black full-length coat.

He didn't need his fifteen years on the force to tell him she was perfectly fine.

And that irritated him. "It's eleven at night. What kind of hours do you keep?"

She had the grace to look guilty, but only slightly. "Some things are more important than sleep. You're a police officer. You should know that."

It was ironic that the girl who'd probably never seen a sunrise was chastising him for being lazy. "I was asleep."

"Well, I haven't gone to bed yet. And…I need some advice."

The concern in her voice kept him from slamming the door in her face. "What happened?" he asked.

A dozen emotions seemed to flit across her face. Pain. Worry. Appreciation. Resolve.

"I saw a boy outside my workplace tonight. His name's Wes. He was collecting cans."

Keaton's interest waned and was replaced by pure disgust. Only his hoity-toity neighbor would be waking him up to file a complaint about a homeless person. Obviously, she had the compassion of a rock. "That's not against the law, Tessa."

She waved a hand. He caught a flash of pink nails. "No! I'm not trying to get *rid* of him. I'm trying to *help*."

Keaton leaned forward and gazed out into the hallway. Though he didn't know her well, he sensed that Tessa McGuiry skated through life without much thought about consequences. He wouldn't put it past her to dump the boy on his doorstep…for him to take care of. "Where is he?"

She blinked twice. "I don't know. With his mom?"

Relieved that he wasn't going to have to deal with anything immediately, he stepped back into his apartment. "If he's with his mom, he's probably okay."

She raised her chin defiantly. "I don't think Wes is okay at all," she said. "*They are living in a car. He was out without gloves. At night. In the sleet.*" After a moment, she added, "I really think we need to do something."

Though there was nothing funny about the situation, he found himself amused by her. She seemed ready to do battle with the world, all five feet of her. His lips twitched. "Oh, you do, do you?" He massaged his scalp, hoping to spur his brain into action. But it didn't help. He'd just come off a twelve-hour shift; *nothing* was going to help him think clearly except sleep. "Let's talk about it in the morning."

"But that's hours from now!"

"You're right. It's late. I should be sleeping."

She crossed her arms over her chest. "Couldn't you go fill out an APB or something?"

Against his will, he almost smiled. It sounded like

Tessa watched too much late-night TV. "This police officer needs his rest. Wait until morning."

"But I—"

He cut her off. "I'll meet you for breakfast at seven at the diner next door. That gives me almost eight more hours to sleep."

"But—"

"Take it or leave it."

With a mutinous look, she said, "I'll take it."

"Excellent. Goodbye." Eager to put some distance between them, he went to push the door shut.

But before he could close it completely, she craned her head around to meet his eyes. "But K—"

Obviously, the woman had never been refused anything before. With his head starting to pound, he said, "'Night, Tessa. I'll see you at breakfast."

Finally, he closed the door and made his way back to bed, exhaustion overtaking his muscles. But though his body was worn out, his mind was already weighing the pros and cons of meeting with Tessa, and worrying about a child walking alone in an alley.

"Hang in there, Wes," he murmured as he crawled between his worn flannel sheets, the ones his wife had bought so long ago. "I'll try and do something." A yawn escaped. He punched the pillow behind his head, recalling how Susan had fluffed the pillows every morning when she'd made the bed.

His eyes drifted shut. A flash of memory brought him to Susan again. This time, she was lying next to him, holding his hand. Rubbing his back so he'd relax. "God, I miss you, Sue," he said.

"ANOTHER CUP OF COFFEE?"

"Maybe a whole carafe, Carla," Tessa mumbled, resting her head in her hands. After stomping down the one flight of stairs to her own apartment, she'd done her best to keep to her regular routine.

She'd taken a bath and put on cozy cotton pajamas. Heated a frozen pizza. Even eaten a couple of spoonfuls of ice cream right out of the container.

But none of her usual cure-alls seemed to make a bit of difference. She'd still felt worried and agitated.

All she'd been able to think about as she was taking her bath was Wes, dirty and cold in his car.

She thought of him eating a couple of cookies while she ate her pizza.

She imagined him and his mom trying to get comfortable in a parking lot while she snuggled deeper under her down comforter.

Her little luxuries now seemed frivolous. Excessive. And she wasn't quite sure what to make of that.

All she really knew was that she needed assistance, and Keaton Phillips, being her neighbor and a cop, was the logical person to approach.

Even though he didn't like her.

She popped her head up when she saw him come through the door, wearing jeans and a crisp button-down under a nylon jacket. "You made it," she said.

"What? You didn't think I would?"

"No, I did. I just..." Her voice trailed off. What could she say that wouldn't embarrass either of them? Not a thing.

He stared at her a moment longer, then with a sigh, sat down.

"Hey, Keaton. Coffee?" Carla asked.

"Yep. Juice, too."

When Carla hurried over with a fresh cup of coffee, he treated her to a smile.

Tessa was dumbfounded. Never, ever, had Keaton smiled at *her* like that. She would have remembered. His smile was perfect. Perfect teeth, perfect jaw...and his green eyes sparkled, too. It completely transformed his craggy face, made him look ten years younger.

Feeling as if she'd been cheated—only ever having received his surliness—she frowned at him.

He noticed. "What?"

"What? I didn't know you could smile, that's all."

"Why would you say that?"

"You've never smiled at me."

"Did you want me to?"

"No."

"Well, then?"

Stung by his aloofness, she changed subjects. "Now, about Wes."

He rolled his eyes. "Unlike you, I actually eat from time to time. We'll discuss this after I get some breakfast."

"I eat."

"Doesn't look like it."

"I had pizza last night."

"What are you having for breakfast?"

She'd been hoping for a pot of coffee. "I don't usually eat breakfast."

"Well, I do."

When Carla came around again, bearing Keaton's juice, Tessa found herself ordering the breakfast special just to spite him.

A few minutes later, their food mercifully arrived.

Keaton didn't seem to need or want conversation. Instead, he concentrated intently on his plate of eggs and bacon, eating with the same kind of precision Tessa figured he brought to target practice and interrogations.

When he was done, he pushed his plate away, took out a notebook and nodded at her.

"Tell me again what happened last night."

She did as he directed, eager to share her story, and felt most of her tension drain away.

Maybe it was because Keaton didn't act surprised to hear that a ten-year-old was collecting cans after dark. The only thing that seemed to catch him off guard was the fact that she'd promised Wes a hundred more cans.

Tapping his pencil, he asked, "So, did you get their license plate?"

"No," she admitted.

"Last name?"

"No."

"Mother's name?"

She was starting to feel ridiculous. "No."

He set his notebook down. "Tessa, I appreciate your trusting me, but even Columbo couldn't do anything with so little information."

"Please," she pleaded. "There has to be something you can do. We know where to look," she said. "In the alleyway behind Sylvia York Designs."

He shrugged. "Who's to say they'll be going back there again? What's happening with Wes and his mom is sad but not all that uncommon. And I'm a cop, not a social worker."

Her shoulders slumped. "Do you know any social workers?"

"I do. And I can give you some names, but I don't think you realize what you're setting yourself up for."

"What do you mean?"

He looked away. "Tessa, if you raise a stink, Wes could be taken away from his mom and put in a foster home. That may not be what either of them wants."

"But what should I do?"

"Collect cans, I guess."

"I can't believe you can joke about this," she said, her frustration causing her temper to rise. "Doesn't his situation affect you at all?"

"Of course it does. But what do you think goes on in this city? Do you really think this boy and his mother are the only ones struggling to eat?"

His sarcasm hurt. “Why don’t you like me?”

He appeared taken aback. “I never said I didn’t like you.”

“Well, it sure seems as if you don’t. Every time we pass each other in the parking lot or in our apartment building, you look the other way.” When he didn’t say anything, she pressed on. “Is it because I dared to complain about your 5:00 a.m. workouts? Because I invited you to the Labor Day mixer? Because I called you ‘antisocial’ that one time?”

His expression turned glacial. “I don’t have time for women like you.”

“Like me, how?”

“You wear designer clothes. You drive a fancy import. You talk a mile a minute and listen with less patience than a two-year-old.”

She hadn’t been around many two-year-olds, but she knew she’d just been insulted. “Anything else?”

“Isn’t that enough?”

“More than enough.”

Pointing at him with her teaspoon, she said, “I guess the women you date are far different.”

A muscle in his cheek twitched. “I don’t date.”

“Maybe you should.” Tessa was fully aware that her voice had become snippy. “Maybe you should get your own life so you can stop judging mine.”

“I used to have one,” he replied quietly. “Until Susan—my wife—died.”

She swallowed hard. “I’m sorry.”

"I am, too." Keaton sighed. "Sorry for what I said. You're right—what you do is none of my business. If Wes comes around again, see if you can get some more information. And I'll talk to a couple of people at the station. Maybe one of them has come in contact with Wes before."

"You'd do that?" she asked.

"I'm not heartless, Tessa. Just a realist."

"Thank you."

He nodded.

Now that they'd reached an uneasy truce, Tessa studied him more closely. Fine lines traced the edges of his eyes, and his broad shoulders looked tense. He appeared exhausted. "Do you have to go into work today?"

"Yeah," he said with a grimace, as he turned his face toward the window. "With the weather like this, a few of us were asked to do some overtime. People drive crazy in the sleet."

"I'm going in, too. We're putting on a fashion show for debutants." Remembering what she'd promised, she asked, "Any idea where I can get sixty cans quickly?"

"For Wes?"

"I promised I'd help him out. It was the only way he'd see me again."

He raised a brow in amusement. "You really want me to be an outstanding public servant, huh?"

She smiled. "Well, yeah."

"You could check the Dumpster behind our building."

She'd been a little afraid she was going to be doing that. Swallowing hard, she said, "Okay."

"Or you could come down to the station with me. We've got a sack full of cans to be recycled. I'll give you as many as you need."

"Really?"

"Like I said, Tessa. I'm not completely heartless."

No, Keaton wasn't completely without a heart, she thought as she followed him out. He cared about Wes, and he cared about other people.

But not her.

Chapter Three

There was no good reason for stopping by Tessa's shop on Monday morning, but Keaton stopped by, anyway. He had two hours before he needed to report for duty, and he wasn't content to sit at home and watch CNN or Headline News—which was unusual for him.

Tessa's appearance and her plea to help Wes had shaken him up, made him feel things that he hadn't felt in a long time. He'd seen a different side of her when he'd escorted her through the station. Far from seeming haughty or awkward, she'd joked with his friends and been genuinely appreciative of the recycled cans he'd given her.

Then, when she'd said goodbye and touched his arm, he'd felt a spark between them. It had caught him by surprise…and made him want to see her again.

After parking in the lot next to the store, he navigated his way around gray mounds of slush to the neatly shoveled sidewalk. The old Victorian building loomed in front of him. Mannequins wearing red and white ball gowns posed in the picture windows. Through the glass, he could see Tessa talking to a well-groomed man in his late twenties, wearing a gray pin-striped suit and a coral-colored tie.

He suddenly felt underdressed in his faded jeans, work boots and snug black turtleneck. What if she took one look at him and forgot their easy camaraderie at the station?

It was certainly possible.

Yeah, there was a very good chance he was going to walk through that door and remember why he'd made a point of avoiding her for so long.

Tessa McGuiry had most likely moved on to the next crisis in her life—a hangnail or something—and he would be left feeling ridiculous. Saddened that she didn't care what happened to a homeless boy anymore.

He almost turned around before he saw her staring right back at him. Smiling, she stepped forward. Knowing there was no turning back, he grasped the door handle.

"Keaton!" she said, as he pulled the heavy door shut behind him. "Do you have news?"

Keaton blinked in an effort to get a grip on his surroundings. The boutique was softly scented with something sweet but not too cloying. Up close, Tessa looked stunning in a raspberry-colored sleeveless dress that had no business being out of the closet in this twenty-degree weather. She wore gold sandals.

Pink toes peeked out at him, and bare legs drew his eyes like a magnet.

Those legs—and that dynamite smile—left his mouth dry. "Uh...no."

"Oh, sorry. I thought you might...since you're here."

Why had he stopped by again? Getting his mind back on his task, he said gruffly, "Remember, I can't help you without more information."

Tessa clutched the hem of her dress for a split second, then smoothed out the crease. "I remember." She stepped closer, lowering her voice as if she didn't want the other guy to overhear. "It's been almost three full days. What do you think has happened?"

He knew he should give her another reality check. But there was something in her hopeful expression—or maybe it was those perfect legs—that made him curb his tongue. "Who knows? It could be anything. Even if the kid wanted to come back, his mother might have had other plans," he said gently.

Shoot. The kid and his mom were probably in another part of the city by now. He should really tell her that.

Her shoulders slumped. "I guess you're right. So, what can I help you with?"

Glancing at the guy in the suit who was making no pretense of ignoring their conversation, Keaton shrugged. "I thought maybe I could take a look out back."

She grinned. "Sure. Hey! Want to see something?"

Without waiting for a reply, she began leading him toward the back room.

There, neatly nestled between two large shelving units and a worn desk, was a clear garbage bag, with dozens of multicolored cans inside.

"If he does stop by again, I'm ready," Tessa said proudly.

Her optimism made him smile. "I guess you are."

She shifted her weight and crossed her arms in front of her chest, as if to guard herself from his criticism. "It's the least I can do to help him. I'm trying, Keaton."

He had to admit he was charmed by her efforts. That her desire to help Wes was obviously sincere.

"If he comes back, I'm sure he's going to be real happy about those cans."

"I hope he does show up so I can get some more information for you," she said. "You'll still help me, right?"

Keaton scanned her face. Noticed how her lips were glossed with some kind of berry-colored lipstick. How her eyes flickered as she waited for his response.

He swallowed. "Yeah, I'll help you."

The nattily dressed young man stuck his head around the door. "Tessa, darling, Mrs. Edwards just pulled in. You'd better get ready to sparkle and shine."

"That's Ryan, my coworker," Tessa explained. "I'd better go. Mrs. Edwards is one of our best customers."

"Sure." He motioned to the back door. "I'll take a look around before I leave."

"Let me know if you find anything." She fluffed her hair and smoothed her dress along her hips. "I'd better get going," she said again, still hesitating.

He tried not to remember what it felt like to run his hands across a woman's body. To feel the soft skin. Pliable, warm.

He stepped back. "Me, too. I've got to—"

"I know. Get to work." She held out her hand. "Thanks for stopping by. I really do appreciate it."

Keaton took Tessa's hand and clasped it. Her skin was smooth and supple, as though she'd never done a hard day's work in her life. But for the first time, he was glad she hadn't. There was something so sweet and feminine about her, he hated the thought of those qualities vanishing. "Let me know if Wes comes back."

"I will."

Ryan poked his head in the room again. "Tessa, are you coming?"

"I'm on my way." Without a backward glance, Tessa stepped quickly from the workroom.

Keaton shook his head and went out into the alley. As he'd expected, it was empty, and he didn't find anything that looked as if it belonged to a boy. He let himself back inside, then walked out into the showroom.

Tessa in her professional capacity looked like a different person to him. Her shoulders were back, her posture perfect. "Mrs. Edwards, these are the new sweaters I was telling you about," he heard her say. "Aren't they lovely?"

Before letting himself out, he glanced at her one last time. She was smiling as if she never thought about anything other than dresses and shoes and selling fancy things to wealthy customers.

Keaton now knew better.

And as he headed back to his six-year-old Jeep, he couldn't quite figure out how he felt about that.

TESSA BIT HER LIP when she realized another day was almost over, and Wes still hadn't returned. Four days had passed, and everything inside her was screaming to move on and stop dwelling on the boy.

She glanced up from the sketch she was doing as Ryan returned from his dinner break, looking as dapper as always in a retro brown plaid suit and suede loafers. "Hey," she said.

"Hey, yourself. Is our lady and mistress here?"

Tessa laughed. "Nope. Sylvia's on a dinner date."

"Good," he said. "I finally remembered to bring you some cans."

He handed her a green shopping bag. In it was an assortment of the cleanest, most precisely crushed cans she'd ever seen. "What do you think?" he asked.

She couldn't resist teasing him. "I think I'm impressed. How'd you get them to look so good?"

"With a meat tenderizer. I found out that if I hit a can just so, it would flatten into a perfect circle."

Tessa didn't dare ask why he found it necessary to make perfect circles. "Thanks."

"You're welcome. Sylvia wants these out of here asap, by the way." He crossed the room, then took the chair next to Tessa. Leaning close, he said, "You know, I was thinking about your Wes, and although I hate to say it, I figure he's probably gone for good. If he was going to come back, he would've by now."

She didn't want to hear that. She hated to think she'd never see Wes again. "He might still come back. At least, I hope he will. I can't stop thinking about how small and cold he looked the other night."

"Oh, I bet he's found someplace warm by now." Ryan wrinkled his nose as he propped a foot on his knee. "Did you see that Kroger's already has artificial Christmas trees? I tell you, pretty soon, people are going to be opening presents before Thanksgiving."

Ryan's deliberate switch in conversation didn't surprise her. He never hid the fact that he'd rather talk about superficial things than anything that really mattered.

"I know what you mean about rushing the season," she said, playing along. "I heard Fountain Square is going to have skating starting Friday."

"Gee. I might even have to take a day off work for that."

"You'd never take off work to skate."

"I would if you would."

Tessa chuckled. Ryan's irreverence was charming,

but she didn't find it as funny as she used to. In fact, just seeing him next to Keaton the day before made her realize he was the complete opposite of her neighbor in almost every way. Ryan rarely strayed beyond his comfort zone…Keaton spent his life on the outskirts of his, helping the community.

Standing up, she said, "Whether or not Wes comes back, we both know Sylvia is going to have me for lunch if I keep strolling around in the alley."

"Come to think of it, Sylvia did ask me why you've been staying late every night," Ryan replied. "She thinks you're working long hours because you want a raise."

"She said that?"

"She did, and I let her think it. I mean, you know how Sylvia is…she thinks everyone always wants something from her." He shrugged. "And, well, I was sure you wouldn't want anything to jeopardize your future here."

"Do you think I should tell Sylvia what I'm doing?" Maybe she wasn't giving Sylvia enough credit…maybe Sylvia did have a heart under all her cashmere and silk.

"It's up to you," he said. "Though we both know that the last thing Sylvia York would want is some hapless, homeless family scavenging in the alley. She doesn't want anyone around who can't buy her stuff." Glancing at the clock above the front door, he softened his tone. "Look at the bright side, Tessa. It's seven o'clock. Pretty soon we'll be going home and you won't have to worry about the kid anymore tonight."

But Tessa knew she would, whether or not she ever saw Wes again. "Mrs. Jackson is due in anytime," she said, fed up with Ryan's attitude. "Please make sure you show her the new suede skirts. I'm going to finish these sketches, then I've got to go over the invoices."

"Gotcha."

She picked up his bag of cans. "Thanks again for these." Then, she strode away before he could say another word.

Two hours passed. Sylvia called, Mrs. Jackson came and went, and finally it was time to lock up.

Ryan pointed to the door. "You want me to take the recycling out to the Dumpster?"

"No," she said. "I'll do it."

Tessa slipped on her coat and gathered up the boxes. As she walked by her sack of squashed cans, she shook her head.

She needed to stop dwelling on the boy.

Maybe it was silly to think she could make a difference by doing something so little. Cans, of all things. Wes needed so much more. Warm clothes, decent food…a home.

And Keaton was right. There were plenty of needy people in the world. If she really wanted to help, she just had to contact the proper authorities and she could do all the charity work she wanted.

So why was she so disappointed that Wes had never come back?

She stepped out into the cold and scanned the alleyway, hoping against hope that he'd be there.

But, of course, he wasn't.

Yep, it was definitely time to call it a night. She hefted the flattened boxes in her arms, their edges almost covering her eyes, and blindly made her way toward the Dumpster.

"Tessa?"

The boxes tumbled out of her hands. "Wes!"

He jumped back. "Yeah."

Tessa felt like hugging him. But, knowing he wouldn't want that, she settled for not even trying to hide her relief. "I was afraid you wouldn't come back."

"I'm here."

"I've got a hundred cans for you."

"You sure?"

"I counted them myself." She peered closely at him. His face was drawn, and his whole posture looked bowed. "Is something wrong?"

He nodded. "My mom's real sick," he said quietly. "I don't know what to do."

The tremor in his voice set her nerves on alert. "Where is she?"

"Over there. We're parked at the end of the alley."

Aware of the potential danger of the situation, Tessa momentarily considered getting Ryan, but she didn't want to risk having Wes run off.

Cautiously, she followed him to the old van.

What if there was no sick mom waiting for them?

What if Wes was just a good actor?

What if he really was scamming her, and there were a couple of thugs in the van, waiting to do who knew what?

Her doubts disappeared at the scene that greeted her. Slumped in the front seat was a woman who could only be Wes's mom. Her wheat-colored hair and brown eyes matched his exactly.

"This is my mom," Wes said. The hitch in his voice told Tessa that he loved the woman very much.

His mom's breathing was labored and she was extremely pale. A band of perspiration lined her brow, although the air was frigid.

"Hello?" Tessa said softly.

Wes's mom barely looked at her.

Wes nudged closer. "Claire," he said. "Her name's Claire. Claire Grant."

She squeezed his shoulder. "Okay." Then, turning to the woman, who couldn't be much older than her, Tessa said clearly, "Claire, I'm Tessa. I think you need to go to the hospital."

After three ragged breaths, Claire replied, "I can't. My boy."

"There's only the two of us," Wes explained.

Tessa knew she was in over her head, but also knew just as strongly that she had to help them. She had no choice. "I'll help with Wes."

At Claire's look of confusion, Tessa added, "I'll go with you to the hospital, and then I'll help with Wes. I promise I'll take care of him for you."

Wordlessly, Wes gazed at her in surprise.

Claire's question was to the point. "Why?"

Tessa thought of her father, leaving the house in the middle of the night when his pager buzzed. Of her brother, a volunteer firefighter. Of how she'd lain awake for four nights, worrying about a little boy she barely knew and feeling completely helpless. "Because I can," she said. "I want to help because I can. Please let me."

Moments passed. Tessa stood rigidly in the cold wind, waiting for Claire's answer, while Wes remained mute, as if he knew his future was out of his hands.

Finally, mercifully, Claire nodded.

The nod spurred Tessa into action. Knowing she was in no position to navigate the icy streets with Wes and Claire in her rear-wheel-drive car, she dug in her coat pocket for her cell phone. "Wes, I'm going to call a friend of mine. His name's Keaton. He'll know what to do."

Luckily, she'd placed his card in her coat pocket two days ago, when she'd been sure Wes was going to return. She punched in his number quickly and prayed he'd answer his cell phone.

"Phillips."

"Keaton? This is Tessa."

"Hey, Tessa. What's up?"

She took solace in his warm tone. "I'm here with Wes and his mom, Claire. She's really sick. She needs to go to the hospital."

He paused. "So, we're now officially involved?"

"And unofficially, too," she said. "Please, Keaton. This is important."

"I know. You at work?"

"Yep."

"I'll be right there. Stay with them."

"I won't go anywhere." As she clicked off, she turned to Wes, who had listened to the exchange with wide eyes.

"Everything's going to be okay. I'm going to do everything I can to make things better. I promise."

Wes said nothing, but did step closer, allowing her to shield him from the night air. Ryan appeared at the back of the store, and Tessa motioned him over. She explained the situation and saw in his face that he thought she'd bitten off more than she could chew.

Then, she closed her eyes and hoped that Keaton would arrive very, very soon.

Chapter Four

The emergency room was crowded. Tessa was grateful that Keaton had arrived within minutes and had taken all three of them to the hospital in his Jeep.

Though having him as an escort had cut through some of the admissions red tape, they'd still waited for at least an hour before Claire had been taken in. Keaton had gone back with her.

Now, sitting quietly with Wes beside her, Tessa realized she might have taken on too much. She didn't have any experience with kids or hospitals. Furthermore, she'd enlisted the help of a man she hardly knew.

Why in the world had she promised Wes that everything was going to be fine?

Tessa felt like some kind of fraud. She was completely out of her depth. Surely someone else should be sitting with Wes. Someone like the calm and efficient police officer who'd met them at admissions.

Tessa had found out afterward that Officer Genevieve Slate was Keaton's partner and was there to give him support.

Though Tessa instinctively knew that Officer Slate hadn't thought much of her, Tessa appreciated her professionalism. It probably would've been better if someone like Officer Slate had been sitting with Wes. Someone who knew how to talk to the hospital administration. Who knew what to do with a ten-year-old. Maybe Tessa should have placed Wes in Officer Slate's capable hands, let her call social services and walked away.

In her heart, she knew that wouldn't have been possible.

She glanced at Wes again. He sat beside her, swinging his legs anxiously as he stared at the stainless steel double doors that led into the triage area.

Knowing how worried she'd be if her own mother was behind those doors, Tessa closed her eyes and tried to think of something to say to him. She had the feeling he wouldn't want to hear any platitudes. Kind words meant nothing if there was no substance behind them.

"Are you hungry?" she finally asked. The instant comfort of a packaged cupcake had gotten her through many a tough time. "There're a couple of vending machines over in the corner. We could go see if they have something you'd like."

He shook his head.

"Hot chocolate?" she offered, now thinking that she, at least, needed the snack. Something to calm her nervous stomach.

When Wes looked as if he was about to refuse again, she said, "I'm going to get some coffee. It'll give us something to do…and warm us up." She followed his gaze, taking in the crying toddler next to them and the elderly man wheezing into a dirty handkerchief. "Your mom's in good hands, you know," she said. "Keaton will make sure of that."

Wes sharpened his gaze. "He's your friend?"

"Yes. I trust him." She and Keaton might not know each other very well, but there was a stalwartness about him. His surliness comforted her. Keaton seemed like the kind of man who would never deliver false promises…he would give her facts and let her be the one to find hope in them.

She nudged Wes's shoulder with her own. "I bet there might even be marshmallows in the hot chocolate. What do you say? Want to give it a try?"

After a pause, Wes finally nodded.

"Will you come help me?"

He nodded again.

Together, they deposited two dollars, then pushed the correct buttons, both watching the machine mix the hot chocolate, then the coffee before their eyes.

"For some reason, I never get tired of watching this," Tessa said, as she opened the plastic door and handed

Wes his drink. "They had one of these machines when I worked at Macy's department store downtown."

Wes took a sip. "It's good, even if there aren't any marshmallows."

"I'm glad." She took a few tentative sips of her coffee. It left much to be desired when compared to the fancy designer blends she was used to, but it did the job. "Mine hits the spot, too."

Almost as if against his will, the corners of Wes's mouth turned up.

Just as they sat back down, Keaton returned from the triage area. He nodded at Tessa, and sat next to Wes, positioning himself so he could meet the boy's gaze directly.

Tessa noticed how strong his hands looked, resting on his thighs, and felt a surge of warmth toward him. "How's Mrs. Grant?" she asked.

"Not so good," he said frankly.

Tessa held her breath as she felt Wes's body tense.

Keaton clasped the boy's shoulder. "Your mom is pretty sick, Wes," he said in his no-nonsense way. "The doctors said you did the right thing by getting help."

Wes didn't look so sure about that. "She's not mad I got Tessa?"

"Not at all."

Tessa sighed. Obviously, this was yet another area where she was completely out of her element. She hadn't even thought to imagine how Wes must be feeling, asking strangers to help his mother...maybe even against her wishes. Something told her that if his mom was living in a car instead of a shelter, she was there by choice.

Wes handed Tessa his still-full cup. "Can I go see her?"

"In a minute." Keaton leaned closer to Wes. "I need to tell you something man-to-man, okay?"

Wes nodded.

"Your mom needs to stay here."

The only response he got from Wes was a further tensing of his slim shoulders.

Tessa hastily put both cups down by her feet. "What did the doctors say?"

Still looking at Wes, Keaton replied, "Your mom has pneumonia and a few other problems, as well. They think she's dehydrated and anemic." He lowered his voice. "She's not going to get much better back in your van, Wes."

"But what…?" Wes's voice drifted off, as if he couldn't bear to ask the questions that were at the front of his mind.

Tessa's heart went out to the boy. She knew what it was like to worry about a sick family member—her brother, James, had been ill with a staph infection back when they both were in college. She remembered how helpless she'd felt as she'd waited with bated breath for the doctor's latest report.

But she had a feeling she knew what else Wes was worried about. "Wes, we can talk to your mom about this, but why don't you spend the night at my apartment? It's late—I'm sure you're tired." When he started to shake his head, she continued quickly. "I have a spare bedroom. You could have your privacy and a warm bed. I'll bring you back here in the morning. Remember? I promised your mom I'd take care of you."

Wes looked at Keaton for reassurance.

Keaton surprised her by nodding. "I already mentioned this to your mom. Since you don't have any relatives living nearby, you can either stay with Tessa or we can call child services."

"I don't know."

Keaton stood up. "Tessa has a real nice place. You'd be safe and get some rest." Meeting Tessa's eye, he added, "If you play your cards right, she might even take you out for breakfast in the morning."

"I think I should be here with my mom," Wes said.

"They're not going to let you stay, son."

Wes stilled. Tessa's heart broke as she saw his bottom lip tremble while he gained control of his emotions. "Sure?"

Keaton nodded. "I'm sure."

"So, can we go visit Claire now?" Tessa asked, seeking to remedy the tense situation.

"Yeah, but only for a minute."

Wes stood. Tessa tossed the cups in the trash, then followed Keaton and Wes through the doors.

"They haven't given your mom a room yet, but

they will," Keaton said, stopping in front of a curtained area. Nodding to the boy, he added, "She's in here. You can go on inside. We'll wait."

Wes didn't need any further prodding. He slipped behind the curtain, leaving Tessa and Keaton standing alone.

"Thank you," she said. "I don't know what I would have done if you hadn't been home."

"You would've done okay. Don't underestimate yourself."

His praise was unexpected, but welcome. "How bad is Claire, really?"

He frowned. "The doctors are still running tests, but from what I understand, it's pretty bad. As far as I can tell, she's been sick for some time. She's underweight and undernourished. It's amazing that Wes looks as healthy as he does...she must've been giving everything she had to him."

"I'm glad you talked with Mrs. Grant about him going to my place."

"Me, too. Thank you for offering it," he murmured, clasping her shoulder in much the same way he had clasped Wes's. "I'll need to contact Child Protection Services and write a report, but for everyone concerned, I think his going home with you, as a friend, is best. The last thing Wes needs right now is to go off with someone he knows even less than the two of us."

Keaton's touch was soothing. "I hope I made the right decision," she said softly.

"I know you did." With a small motion, he curved his hand and brushed the bare skin of her neck, his eyes gentling when a tremor coursed through her. "Right now, what he needs most is to get some rest, and the best thing for his mom is to know that he's okay."

Slowly, she turned to him, a thousand questions running through her head—only they weren't all about Wes. She wanted to know if he felt the connection between them, too… If he, also, wanted to forget about their past disagreements and get to know each other better.

"Tessa?" Wes called through the curtain.

"Yes?" she asked, all thoughts of Keaton and their relationship vanishing.

"Can you come in here?"

Tessa gingerly entered the enclosed area, Keaton following close behind her. As she pulled the curtain to one side, Tessa was shocked to see how poorly Claire looked now that she was cleaned up and in a hospital gown. The lack of layers emphasized just how thin and ill she was. She glanced at Wes's face to see how he was handling it. His mouth was pinched and he appeared noticeably paler.

Putting her best smile on, she said, "Hi, Claire. I heard you're going to keep those doctors busy for a little while."

"So I hear," she whispered, after an obviously painful swallow.

Wes bit his lip.

After sharing a concerned look with Tessa, Keaton spoke. "It's late. I think it would be a good idea if Wes went home with Tessa. Wes could take a hot shower and get some rest. Would that be okay with you? Tessa is my neighbor, she lives just below me. So, if he needs anything, I could lend a hand, too."

Claire nodded. "All right."

Wes clutched his mother's hand. "You sure, Mom? I could wait here."

"I'll rest better if I know you're sleeping in a bed, sweetie," she said with visible effort.

A nurse popped her head in. "We're almost ready to take Ms. Grant for more tests. It's time to go."

"I'll call later to see how things are going," Keaton said to Tessa.

She turned to Wes. He was still holding his mother's hand and didn't seem ready to release it any time soon. As gently as possible, she asked, "What do you think? Can we let your mom visit with the doctors and get some rest?"

Wes looked at his mother, who nodded. "I guess so."

Tessa wrote down her cell phone number and her home phone, as well, before placing the paper on the table beside Claire's bed. "We're only a phone call away. We'll be back tomorrow."

Claire was prevented from answering when a thick cough racked her body.

"It's time to go," Keaton said.

The three of them left just as a team of nurses and

professionals entered the cubicle. Wes looked as if he was about to cry.

Keaton put his arm around the boy's shoulders and steadily guided him through the medical maze and back to the exit.

"How about I take the two of you home, then get someone to drive your car over? It's still at work, right?"

"It is. That would be great."

"What do you think, sport? Want to sit up front with me, or in the back?"

Wes shrugged.

Keaton's voice gentled. "Letting your mother stay here on her own is what she needs. Sometimes we have to think of what's best for other people."

"I know," Wes said quietly as he climbed into the front seat of Keaton's Jeep. "But it's still hard."

"You're right, it is," Keaton whispered. "Let's head on home."

Tessa leaned her head on the back of the seat and closed her eyes. What a night.

Wes had finally returned and brought with him so much more than she'd counted on. It was amazing that she'd gone from collecting cans for him to opening up her home. But, the offer had felt right—and it still did, she thought, as she looked at Wes, slumped beside Keaton. They'd all done the right thing by that boy.

Glancing from Wes to Keaton, and observing how strong and sure Keaton seemed next to the little boy, she felt a warmth of another kind. Friendship. She wouldn't have to worry about accidentally running into Keaton Phillips in her apartment complex anymore. They were partners now. Or, at least, almost friends.

She was looking forward to investigating the spark of anticipation she felt whenever they were together. Yes, her life had just taken a new turn.

She hoped and prayed she was steering it in the right direction.

Chapter Five

With Wes in bed and Tessa fixing a snack in the kitchen, Keaton let himself sink into Tessa's cushiony couch. The down-filled pillows cradled his neck and a small voice inside him hinted that he should be finding fault with the expensive piece of furniture. After all, it was the exact opposite of something Susan would have bought.

Susan had always been aware of their finances. Everything she'd purchased had been solid, built to last and easy to clean.

The sofa he was sitting on was none of those things.

Ever since his run-in with Tessa over his workout schedule, he'd searched for things to find fault with her: her car, her completely unsensible shoes. The way she never seemed to walk anywhere without a cell phone attached to her ear. How she always managed to look good, even when she was working out in their fitness room…if you could call it working out. Tessa seemed to think working out meant putting on coordinated jogging outfits and walking lazily on the treadmill for fifteen minutes, all the while chatting with whoever was in there.

And then there were all the guys she dated. Men with too much money and too much time. They picked her up at all hours and took her home way too late—not that it was any of his business.

Not that he cared.

She'd only caught his attention because she was so different from his wife.

So different from himself. She was constantly smiling. Her laughter echoed through their walls. Her vivaciousness was the exact opposite of how he was feeling: listless.

But now, after seeing how she'd comforted Wes at the hospital and offered him her home, Keaton was struck once again by how much more there was to her than he'd originally thought.

Tessa McGuiry had a good heart—even if her cheekbones were too pretty and her eyes too blue.

And she sure knew how to decorate a place.

He shifted positions, sighing with pleasure as he propped his feet up on the coffee table.

"I see you've made yourself comfortable," Tessa said. She was carrying two mugs of decaf coffee and two slices of apple pie on a tray.

He sat up. The muscles in his back screamed in pain.

Her brow wrinkled. "What's wrong?"

"Nothing. My back—I'm just getting old."

"I sometimes feel that way myself," she said with a wry grin, placing a piece of pie and a mug in front of him, then joining him on the couch. "I'm glad you wanted some dessert."

"I never refuse free food."

"Me neither," she quipped. "I'm one of those people who's always looking forward to the next snack."

Devoid of heels and with her hair in disarray, she looked younger and almost approachable. Keaton couldn't help noticing how her skirt rode up on her thighs as she tucked one foot underneath her.

He knew he should look away but couldn't. Not when he caught a flash of bare skin through the buttonholes of her blouse. Not when the faint scent of her perfume drifted toward him, awakening senses that had been dormant for two long years.

He needed to get a grip. He had no business thinking about her in a romantic way. Okay, a sexual way.

Grief still woke him up some nights. The memory of getting the phone call that Susan had been in an accident…of racing to the hospital but being too late. Of seeing his wife in a way that no husband should ever see.

That night, he'd promised himself he'd love Susan forever. So, why couldn't he stop thinking about Tessa's lithe figure?

"How's Wes?" he asked, steering the conversation in a safe direction.

She glanced down the hall at the closed bedroom door. "I think he's going to be okay. At least for tonight."

Keaton smiled, recalling how the boy had jumped at the opportunity to take a hot shower. He'd also seemed excited about the novelty of having a room to himself…and about the police academy T-shirt Keaton had promised to bring him tomorrow.

"I think *you're* going to be okay, too," he said, wanting to erase the worry lines that had suddenly appeared around Tessa's lips. "Sitting with that boy in the waiting room, giving him a place to stay—what you've done is pretty incredible."

"You think so? It doesn't seem like much. I…I've never done anything like this. I've never done more for the homeless than give them a few dollars. I've certainly never opened my home to a stranger." She played with the hem of her skirt, avoiding his eyes. "You probably think that's pretty bad, huh?"

"No. It's not like cops are in the business of opening up their homes, either."

She gave him a small smile. "I guess you're right."

Finally giving in to his desire to touch her, Keaton squeezed her shoulder. "No matter what happens, you did the right thing tonight. You should feel good about that."

KEATON'S TOUCH SENT A WEALTH of emotions rushing through Tessa. His thinking she'd done the right thing was comforting. Wes and Claire had needed a helping hand, and luckily, she and Keaton had been there for them tonight.

It was strange how her relationship with her neighbor had changed so drastically, so quickly. Now, it was impossible to think of him as *just* an acquaintance. There was a connection between them.

Even if they didn't have anything in common. Even if wanting to help the Grants was the only thing they shared.

She couldn't ignore how motherly she'd felt, doing her part, as well. After letting Wes eat an extra-big helping of ice cream while he watched the cartoon channel, she'd walked him to the guest bedroom. He'd crawled into bed without a second's hesitation and sleepily told her good night.

He'd been so trusting. Obviously, the boy had been exhausted.

But, he'd still looked to *her* for help. Had he seen more in her than she'd dared to see in herself since going to work for Sylvia? A part of her that cared about more than a prestigious career?

She certainly hoped so.

Keaton placed a pillow under his back. "I can't believe how much that kid ate. What did he have? Something like three grilled cheese sandwiches?"

Tessa nodded. "He had a whole can of tomato soup, too." Thinking how grateful he'd been for the simple meal, she said, "I don't cook much. I'm glad he's not picky."

"I imagine he's learned not to be."

She met his gaze, then swallowed any comment she was about to make. His eyes were calming, almost magnetic. She took in the rest of him. His square jaw. His crooked nose that looked as if it had been broken one too many times. His broad chest and shoulders.

He was the type of man no one messed with, and she was sure he wouldn't put up with it if someone tried. No, Keaton Phillips wasn't the kind of guy who looked to other people to help solve his problems. He solved them himself.

Keaton stretched again, his biceps under his black turtleneck flexing with the motion. Her body responded with a pang of awareness.

Hastily, she sipped more of her coffee.

As if he felt the same thing she did, Keaton took another bite of pie. "Now, even a picky eater would enjoy this pie."

"Thank you," she said.

"Did you make it?"

The idea that he thought she could produce such a tasty concoction made her grin. "No way. I rarely have time to bake, and so far, my efforts have centered around Betty Crocker cake mixes." She speared a portion of the crust. "This pie is way beyond my talents. I bought it at the bakery down the street from work. I buy so much there, I'm afraid I could single-handedly keep them in business."

"You have a sweet tooth?"

"I'm afraid it's more like a lot of sweet teeth. There isn't much I wouldn't do for a really good chocolate chip cookie."

Keaton was charmed. Susan had made everything from scratch. He'd come home every night to an appetizing dinner—and some, especially in the beginning of their marriage, that weren't quite so appetizing.

"What are you smiling about?"

"Oh, nothing." How could he even begin to explain the contradictory feelings he was having? How he both missed Susan's domestic talents and found Tessa's lack of them endearing?

She cocked an eyebrow. "You sure? I could use something to smile about."

He shifted. For the first time since he could remember, he was reluctant to talk about his wife. The feeling was novel—and strange. He usually clung to her memory like a life preserver. "It's nothing. I was just thinking about my wife. When we first got married, she made these elaborate dinners that were horrible."

Instead of acting perturbed that he'd brought up Susan, Tessa looked genuinely intrigued. "Somehow, I imagine you didn't give her too much grief."

"Not too much," he murmured. No, he'd loved every one of her attempts to please him. She made him feel special, loved.

"And I bet, like a good husband, you ate every bite," Tessa added, somewhat mischievously.

"No," he said with a laugh. "The chicken would be so dry it could be mistaken for sawdust. Or so raw that you'd be worried about salmonella." He shook his head. "She managed to burn every casserole, I don't know how."

"So, what would you do?"

"We'd make dinner over again. It cost a fortune." He'd been so stressed about money in those days. Stressed, but not willing to sacrifice Susan's feelings. "One day—out of the blue—she got the hang of it."

"You're lucky you had her," Tessa said softly.

Although Keaton knew her words came from her heart, they hit him wrong. "I don't think lucky is the right way to put it. Susan died before she was thirty."

Tessa's cheeks paled. "I just meant you're lucky to have been so much in love."

He knew he should apologize to her. It wasn't Tessa's fault Susan had died in a car accident. The fault belonged to the drunk driver who hit her.

Susan died, the driver was sentenced to ten years for involuntary manslaughter, and Keaton was given a life sentence: to go on living without his wife.

"I don't know if I was lucky. How can I be lucky if my marriage only lasted a few years?"

"At least you got to experience what a good relationship is like," Tessa said. "Me, I've never had a relationship that lasted more than a few weeks."

Keaton thought about all the different men he'd seen her with. Maybe she dated so much because she was looking for love, not just a good time. "I'm finding out that lasting relationships are few and far between. My partner, Gen, says that all the time."

"I agree with her there. It's come to the point where I can determine whether a guy is relationship material within ten minutes of conversation."

"Susan and I met when we were young," Keaton said. "When you get older it seems to me you have to work harder at finding someone."

Tessa nodded. "It's true, and it doesn't help that not too many single men shop at S.Y.D."

"Do you like your job?"

"Of course I do."

"Why?" Keaton blurted before he thought better of it.

Tessa shrugged. "I don't know. Because I'm good at it, I guess."

"You looked happy when I stopped by the other day."

"When I'm there, I shine," she said, a little defensively. "I feel good about myself. I know I'm a valuable asset."

"I know what you mean. I've always felt that I was meant to be a cop."

"I've got a lot of responsibility at the store," Tessa continued, sounding as if she was trying to convince both of them of her job's importance. "I manage the boutique and run it on a day-to-day basis. Customers appreciate my advice." She shrugged again. "I come from a family of people who do great things for other people. So, even though I'm not exactly saving lives…it's where I fit in."

"That's good."

"It is," she said, but her voice sounded wistful.

"I'll get the Grant's van taken to a lot behind the station," Keaton said, switching the topic. "Two uniforms are dealing with your car. I'll drop off your key in the morning so they don't wake you. I guess you'll be checking in on Claire at the hospital tomorrow."

Tessa blinked. "Oh. Yes." She stood up. "Well, I'd better go to bed. It's been a long night."

"What are you going to do about work?"

"I'll call in sick."

"Your boss isn't going to have a problem with that?"

"She won't have much of a choice. We do get sick days… I've just never taken one before."

Keaton nodded and stood, as well. For a brief moment, he considered giving her a hug, then immediately thought the better of it.

It would be best if they kept things professional. Businesslike.

He walked to the door. "Good night, Tessa."

"'Night," she said. *Did he imagine the tone of regret in her voice?*

Shaking his head as he climbed the stairs to his own apartment, Keaton thought how glad he was that he hadn't done anything he'd regret. He'd had a relationship—and it had been great. He didn't need another one.

Especially not with someone like Tessa.

Chapter Six

"Mrs. Grant has several complications. Her lungs are retaining fluid, her fever is high and her blood pressure is elevated. The antibiotics should kick in soon, but they haven't yet."

With a sigh, Dr. Jacobson removed his wire-rimmed glasses and rubbed his eyes. "I'd say she's going to need to be hospitalized for at least another two to three days," he said. "Perhaps even a week, or longer. In addition, I'm hesitant to release Mrs. Grant until her social worker can find her a safe place to go. If she continues to live the way she has, all our efforts will be for nothing."

Wes's grip stiffened in Tessa's hand and she could feel him getting upset. "It's okay," she said.

"No, it's not."

Dr. Jacobson crouched down and put a hand on Wes's shoulder. "You're right, son, it's not okay. But we'll make it better."

Gently rubbing the boy's back, Tessa said, "One day at a time, okay? I'll talk to the social worker. We'll find a place for you both to live."

A glimmer of hope, clouded by doubt, entered his eyes. "You think you'll be able to?"

"We'll do our very best." Tessa struggled to keep her voice even. It was a crime that such a young boy had so many things to worry about.

"You can go see your mom now," Dr. Jacobson said. Wes shrugged before quietly entering his mother's room.

His maturity made her realize she'd done the right thing. She'd considered shielding him from the doctor's report but had decided he and his mother had been taking care of each other for a long time; it would've been unfair to pretend that he couldn't shoulder the weight of Claire's illness after all they'd been through.

Tessa watched Wes walk away, and then the doctor turned to her. "Any questions?"

"No. I'll talk to Mrs. Grant and contact social services. I know Officer Phillips is working on it, too."

"For the record, I think what you've done for them is commendable."

"I'm not doing anything any decent person wouldn't have done."

"You'd be surprised," the doctor said.

"Wes is a good kid. Thanks for everything you've done."

Dr. Jacobson smiled. "You're welcome, Miss McGuiry."

"Tessa."

"Tessa." Gently, he squeezed her arm. "It wouldn't hurt you to get some rest, as well."

"I'll try."

"See that you do." He walked away, leaving Tessa with the feeling that all of the Grants' problems were resting uncomfortably on her shoulders.

She peeked into Claire's room and saw Wes and his mom talking quietly to each other. Wes's face was animated, and he appeared to be relaying everything he'd done in the last twenty-four hours.

Knowing they needed a few more minutes of privacy, she walked over to a pair of aqua vinyl chairs and sat down. Heeding the doctor's advice, she tried to relax. It was difficult, though.

As she'd suspected, Sylvia hadn't been happy when Tessa had called that morning. In fact, she'd pretty much threatened to fire her if she'd didn't come back to work by the following Monday.

Tessa had hated listening to her tirade, hated the warring emotions it stirred up. She cared about Wes and his mom—but she also cared about her job. The thought of losing everything she'd worked so hard for wasn't easy to swallow. There was no way she was giving up her job without a fight.

She needed to find a shelter for Claire and Wes to live. Her place was too small for the three of them, and Claire was going to need someone to help her while she got better.

And then there was school. That morning, Wes had confided that he'd missed the last two days of school and was anxious about missing even more. Tessa knew it had to be her priority to get him back to his normal routine, but even if he was in school, she'd still have to work it out with Sylvia so she could drop him off and pick him up afterward.

"I thought I'd find you here," Keaton said, coming toward her. He was in full uniform, a novelty for her. When she'd seen him around their apartment complex before, he'd always been in khakis and a button-down.

But today, his dark blue uniform emphasizing his solid build, he looked dark, handsome…and pretty darn irresistible. Obviously, there really was some truth to the saying about a man in uniform.

"You look nice," she blurted out, then shut her mouth quickly. Great. Now he was going to think she was flirting with him. Just what he wouldn't want.

He flashed a smile. "Thanks. Everyone got pushed into service this morning—the governor's in town and more than a couple of groups hinted they might protest. So, any news?"

"Unfortunately, yes." Briefly, she outlined what the doctor had said.

Keaton sat down on the chair next to her, and Tessa couldn't resist examining his badge, a medal of commendation pinned below it. She wondered how he'd earned it. If he'd been injured. Keaton was so stoic about his work on the force. Rarely did he talk about what he did, seeming to prefer to focus on her. "Thanks for stopping by," she said.

"You're welcome. Where's Wes?"

"With his mom."

His expression grave, he asked, "You going to be able to keep him for a few days?"

Something in his eyes gave her pause. She sensed he only wanted to hear a truthful answer. No bravado.

Here was her opportunity to say no. To hand over the responsibility to Keaton. He'd deal with Wes and wouldn't think any less of her—after all, he already thought she was shallow. What would it matter if she simply confirmed it? It wasn't as if they really had a relationship.

But, as far as saying she couldn't look after Wes anymore—there was no way she could do that. She cared about the boy too much. He was scrappy and tough…and vulnerable.

That morning, when she'd made him toast and eggs, he'd acted as if she'd served him a plate of eggs Benedict. He drank his instant hot chocolate like it had been made with milk and Ghirardelli.

And when he'd emerged from his shower the night before, looking and smelling so fresh, he'd seemed like a little boy again. Her heart had swelled in her chest when he put on his clothes that morning and said they felt all soft and warm.

She knew she'd do nothing but worry about him if she let Keaton place him with somebody else. She didn't have a choice.

"I'll watch him as long as he needs me," she said.

"You sure?"

"Positive."

"Good. I think the kid is going to need as many people helping him out as possible."

"Why do you say that?"

He leaned toward her, his cologne infusing the antiseptic-smelling hallway with a woodsy scent. "When I was filing my report, I went ahead and did some checking on Claire."

"And?"

"What I found wasn't good."

Tessa's heart thudded as Keaton pulled out a computerized police report.

Chapter Seven

Keaton had steeled himself before sharing the contents of the police report with Tessa. She was already emotionally involved with the Grant family and could take what he was about to tell her hard.

As a police officer, he'd learned that a person either had to become detached if he wanted to stay sane or never sleep at night. There were too many people with too many problems for one man to solve. Too many people who did bad things that didn't make sense. The sheer evil in the world boggled his mind.

If one person tried to fix every predicament he came across, all he'd end up with was a load of regrets.

Susan's death was a prime example. What happened to her shouldn't have ever occurred. But if he stewed on it, he would only hurt worse and lose more sleep. Keaton knew it was best to move on, to take another step forward with his life, just as the counselors at the station had encouraged him to do.

"Would you mind translating this report?" Tessa asked, prompting him out of his reflection. "All I see is a bunch of legalese."

"First off," Keaton said, "it looks like Claire's husband died a little over a year ago. From what we've been able to piece together, he died after an altercation in one of those pool halls down in Newport."

Surprise and empathy filled Tessa's gaze. "And?"

"And Gen and I discovered that before he died he'd run up thousands of dollars in credit-card debt." Pointing to the sheet, he added, "It's obvious Claire's in a deep financial hole, but we're still making our way through the specifics. Most of the cards were in Ray Grant's name, so Claire won't be responsible."

"Do you think she knew what her husband was doing?"

Keaton shrugged. "A lot of people these days are living paycheck to paycheck and taking advantage of easy credit. It isn't that unusual."

"But is Claire in danger of being arrested?"

"Nah. From what I can see, she hasn't done anything wrong. The credit-card companies might file a civil suit, asking for payments, but that's about all."

"From the dates on your report, it looks as if Claire and Wes have been living in a downward spiral for some time."

Keaton nodded. "Yeah. The kid's definitely had a tough time of it. A lot of Ray's problems died with him, but the ramifications hit Claire and Wes hard.

She couldn't afford her apartment, then lost her job because she had no phone or residence. I think she's been cleaning houses while Wes has been at school, but then that got to be too much when she got sick."

"I feel so sorry for her. What about all the money her husband owed?" Tessa whispered. "Is she going to have to pay it back?"

Keaton shrugged. "The credit companies might try to sue her for the money owed, but it wouldn't affect the police department. Neither Gen nor I could find any record of her being an accessory to a crime."

"And if she does get sued?"

Keaton shrugged. "She'll either need to file for bankruptcy or work with a loan company."

"So things are going to get better for her now, right?"

"Hopefully. I contacted Janet Hughes. She's a top-notch social worker who I've worked with before. She's going to help Claire make some decisions when she gets better." Resting his elbows on his knees, Keaton added, "She's going to need a lot of support."

Suddenly, Tessa felt the weight of her actions hit her hard. When she'd set out to help Wes, all she'd thought about were his immediate needs. When she'd seen how ill his mom was, she'd only thought about getting her to the hospital.

She'd never imagined she'd be worrying about Claire's credit-card debt or how to take care of a ten-year-old.

Shaking her head, she said, "Keaton, I don't know

what to do," and immediately regretted it when the warmth in his eyes dissipated.

"I can give Janet a call now. I'm sure she can take Wes off your hands today, if that's what you want."

Why did he constantly think the worst of her? "That's not what I meant," she said.

She was about to try and explain herself more clearly when Wes peeked out the door. "Tessa?" he asked, his voice small. "My mom wants to see you."

Wearily, Keaton walked out into the chilly weather, blinking as his eyes teared up from the cold.

His cell phone started ringing the minute he got in his cruiser. "Phillips."

"Hey, officer. Want to grab a cup of coffee with me?" his partner, Genevieve, asked.

He smiled in spite of himself. Genevieve's coffee breaks were euphemisms for lunch, donut breaks or a quick burger at a diner. She could eat more than any man he knew and still had the kind of lanky, slim figure most women would kill for.

Gen's no-nonsense demeanor was exactly what Keaton needed right now. Hopefully, she'd help take his mind off Tessa and the way she'd glared at him before she'd left. Glancing at his watch, he figured he could spare thirty minutes before he went back to the station.

"Sure," he told Genevieve. "Where do you want to go?"

"Kamon's?"

Keaton winced. "You sure you're up for a greasy burger? Last time we ate there, I had to buy two packs of Tums."

"You're such a lightweight."

He tried to compromise. "Capital Tavern?"

"Ick. All they have there are salads and soup."

"They have sandwiches, too. And besides, some vegetables might be good for you. I'd bet you haven't eaten anything green in days."

"You'd lose that one. I ate two pickles yesterday."

He grinned, knowing she was scowling into the receiver, and played his last card. "They serve corn bread with the soup. Real butter, too."

"Oh...all right. I'll see you there."

When Keaton pulled into the tavern's parking lot, Genevieve was getting out of her car.

Just to tease her, he said, "I think you'd better start laying off those donuts. There's a rumor going around that you can't keep up with some of the new recruits."

Genevieve mock-laughed, and Keaton held the tavern door for her. Built during the turn of the last century, the Capital was known for its history, monster salads and delicious vegetable soup. It was a good spot to eat quickly on a dime.

After they'd ordered their food, Genevieve leaned forward and gazed at him over folded hands. "How are things going at the hospital?"

"Mrs. Grant is still doing poorly." With a frown, he added, "I told Tessa about the information we dug up."

"How'd she take it?"

"Not so well."

"I'm not surprised. From what you've told me about her, it sounds like this whole situation is way out of her league."

Feeling compelled to stand up for Tessa, Keaton said, "I've gotten to know her, and she may be in a little over her head, but I think her offer to take care of Wes is pretty commendable."

Gen whistled, a new light shining in her eyes—Keaton wasn't sure if it was amusement or dawning respect. "I never knew you were such a softie. Care to take on my great aunt? She's got a whole host of problems, including four neurotic parakeets."

"Hey, I'm not trying to save the world."

Pushing a stray hair from her long ponytail away from her cheek, she murmured, "Only Claire and her kid. Does your interest in this case have anything to do with your neighbor, by any chance?"

He wasn't sure if he could put into words why he was so involved. But as he was trying, Genevieve spoke again.

"Are you thinking about asking her out? Where would you take her? She probably only dines at five-star restaurants."

The jealous tone in his partner's voice disturbed him.

"You read through the case file with me. It's obvious this boy could use some extra attention and obvious that it's easier on everyone involved to let Tessa watch him instead of placing him in a complete stranger's home. I'm just trying to do what's right. It has nothing to do with Tessa or her—" He stopped himself before he said something he'd regret.

"Are you sure?"

"I think so," he conceded.

"It sounds as if Tessa's gotten under your skin." Flashing him an uncharacteristically feminine smile, Gen added, "Are you finally ready to start living again, Phillips?"

Keaton knew a flirtatious invitation when he heard it. Suddenly, all those times he and Genevieve had had pizza together or caught a movie took on new meaning. He'd always thought of her as a kind of sister—but could it be that she hadn't looked at him in the same way?

Keaton swallowed a fortifying spoonful of his soup. How had he never seen Gen's motives for what they were? And what was it about Tessa that was so different from Genevieve? Tessa *had* gotten under his skin. He struggled for something to tell Gen, without giving away too much. "Tessa's okay. There's more to her than a pretty face. She's taken on Wes.... That's more than most people would do. You know that."

Genevieve sobered. "I do. But my guess is that her newfound helpfulness is going to get old quick. It probably won't be long before she gets irritated with the kid for putting a crimp in her society lifestyle." Gesturing with her knife, she continued, "You know what I mean…she's going to be stuck with him and she won't be able to get her nails done at the salon anymore."

"I think she caters to society ladies more than she *is* one," Keaton replied.

"She probably aspires to be one of them. Most women do."

"Is that right? Do you?" He leaned back as she stared at him in horror.

"No, I don't," she said firmly and emitted a bark of laughter. "Can you imagine me in a skirt, Keaton?"

Actually he couldn't…but he couldn't help acknowledging that he liked how Tessa looked in one.

His partner smirked. "I bet right this minute Tessa's calling everyone she knows, trying to get her life back to how it was."

Keaton had just about had enough of Gen's criticism. "She's not like that," he said curtly, thinking he should've come to that realization earlier, when Tessa had admitted she was feeling overwhelmed.

For a moment, it looked as if Gen was going to add something else, but she only shook her head.

A feeling of momentary concern passed through him. As partners and friends, he and Genevieve had been there for each other countless times. He didn't want this thing with Tessa to come between them.

"Have you seen *Flight From Beyond?*" he asked in a deliberate attempt to lighten their conversation.

They both enjoyed the movies. Especially action ones, where they could dissect the director's flaws.

"Nope." Brightening, she asked, "Want to go soon? I'm off Monday night."

"Sure."

"It's a date."

The word caused a warning bell to go off in his head. The tone of her voice insinuated it could be a real one.

"Sure," he said. He was about to say something about how he was glad they were *partners* when his radio beeped.

"Just in time," Genevieve replied cryptically, leaving Keaton to wonder if she'd just read his mind.

Chapter Eight

"I don't know why I need all these clothes," Wes complained from his side of the dressing room door. "Trying on stuff is boring."

"It's necessary. How are those jeans fitting?"

"I don't know."

Tessa bit her lip and prayed for patience. Ever since they'd visited his mom, Wes had been argumentative and sullen. "Want to let me see?"

"No."

Feeling as frustrated as Wes sounded, Tessa crossed her arms. "Wes, you need a couple of changes of clothes. And pajamas. And shoes."

"I don't need pajamas. I have Keaton's academy shirt. He said I could wear that."

He did look cute in Keaton's old T-shirt, Tessa thought, but it would hardly keep out the cold. "Don't you think you need something warmer?"

"No. I like his shirt. Why can't I wear it?"

His last sentence had come out as a whine. As several women gave her knowing looks, Tessa took a deep breath and counted to ten. "Wes, what's wrong?" she asked, her voice rough with exasperation. "You know I'm only trying to help you."

After a lengthy pause, she heard a sob.

"Hey, are you okay?" she asked, approaching the door.

"N-n-no."

"Let me in?"

To her relief, Wes twisted the handle. When she entered, Tessa found him wearing a new fleece sweatshirt, but he still had on his old jeans. One shoe was against the wall, the other on his foot, the lace in a knot. Thick tears traced lines down his cheeks.

When he met her gaze, his shoulders shook. "My mom should be here," he cried, going readily into Tessa's outstretched arms.

"I know," she said, kneeling down and hugging him close. "I'm sorry she's not."

"It's not fair."

No, it wasn't. Wes shouldn't have to be shopping for clothes with a strange woman. He shouldn't have to worry about his mom in the hospital.

He shouldn't have had to live in a van for the last three months.

Tessa rubbed his back and let him cry. When his tears subsided, he stepped back and wiped off his cheeks with his fist.

"I don't know how to make everything better," she whispered, finding it easier to admit the truth to Wes than to Keaton. "But, I do know that if you're dressed warm, your mom won't worry about you being cold."

With a ragged sigh, he nodded.

"Can I help you with your shoe?"

"I can't get the knot out."

"I'll get it," she said, quickly loosening the knot with her long nails.

After she got his shoe off, he mumbled, "I want to sleep in Keaton's shirt."

"All right," she said, giving in. "I think that would make Keaton very happy."

Raising his chin, he added, "I'll get the jeans and stuff."

"I'm glad."

Stepping out of the dressing room, Tessa closed her eyes. She was doing the best she could. She hoped it was good enough…at least for today.

"NOW, TESSA, I'M SURE YOU know I have *very* strong concerns about what you're telling me," Sylvia said late Friday afternoon, peering over a pair of rhinestone reading glasses. "I believe you've gotten your priorities confused."

Tessa groaned inwardly. The whole time they'd been talking, Sylvia had either been fiddling with the frames or using them as a makeshift pointer. The fake glasses seemed to be a perfect illustration of her boss's personality, their over-accessorized exterior cloaking a deficient core.

"In fact, I'm having trouble understanding why it's so difficult for you to remember what's important. Priorities, Tessa," her boss repeated, propping those frames on her head to stem her cascade of long blond hair.

Three years ago when Tessa had been hired at S.Y.D., she'd felt so lucky to be working for such a well-known designer and socialite. But now, all she could see was how ridiculous Sylvia seemed, using glasses as a fashion statement when there were so many people who needed corrective eyewear but couldn't afford it.

Because Tessa knew that Wes was with Keaton and that both of them needed to get some sleep soon, she tried once more to explain herself. "Sylvia, I'm only going to be working abbreviated hours for a few more days."

"Yes, but I need you here full-time. Shipments are arriving. Orders have to be placed." Pushing the frames back on the bridge of her nose, Sylvia gazed down at her through them. "Have you forgotten that this time of year is our busiest? Our customers aren't happy that you're taking time off."

Sylvia's office had never felt so small. "I realize now is a hectic time, but pretty much every month is crazy. I'm sure our customers would understand if I took a little time off for personal reasons."

"I doubt it. Most of them are used to being waited on hand and foot."

"Perhaps we should hire more help."

"What? And fire them when you feel ready to come back? That's not exactly fair, is it? You're going to have to rethink your priorities."

That was exactly what she'd been doing. But, because she still needed her job for the moment, Tessa tried another tack. "When I was hired, I believe I was promised two weeks' vacation. You and I both know I haven't taken more than two days off in the last year."

Her boss leaned forward, delicately resting her elbows on her thighs. "Tessa, darling. I'm not asking you to do a thing that I'm not. We both know that I haven't taken a vacation day, either."

No, Sylvia just managed to work in Paris, London and New York City for extended periods of time.

"I'm sorry, but I don't feel I have a choice," Tessa said.

"Everyone has a choice, dear."

She was not Sylvia's dear. The pet name grated her, almost as much as their unnecessary conversation did. "This boy needs me."

"So do I." A sudden spark entered Sylvia's eyes. "Do you remember the conversation we had six months ago? How I was considering giving you a raise? These days off just might put that in jeopardy."

This was harsh, even for Sylvia. The raise she had alluded to would have been enough to make Tessa's dream of opening her own boutique a real possibility. But her instincts told her that if working sixty to seventy hours a week hadn't earned her the extra money, giving up her principles wouldn't, either.

Switching subjects, Tessa said, "I thought I'd talk to Ryan and Jillian tonight and answer any questions they might have, and I'll pop in next week while Wes is at school. There's also a children's club at the hospital, so maybe Wes can go there for a little bit. But I won't be able to work anywhere near the hours you're used to."

"Well, thank goodness Ryan has said he's willing to work overtime. He needs to spend a certain numbers of hours interning in a managerial capacity for his college program. It should serve him well."

Sylvia's statement hung in the air, daring Tessa to question her intent. "I guess you'll have to decide what you want to do," Tessa said simply.

"I guess I will." Clutching her purse, Sylvia moved toward the door. "I have several errands I'd best get done before you take off." She gave one last hard stare, then grabbed her mink and left.

Tessa leaned back in her chair, exhausted. She heard applause, and Ryan appeared in the doorway of the office. "Bravo, Tessa," he said. "I must say, from what I managed to hear, you were incredible."

"No thanks to you."

His eyes widened in mock surprise. "What do you mean by that?"

"I mean you could have come in here and helped me out."

"What could I have said? That you deserve some time off because you suddenly have a desire to help the needy?"

"That's not fair," she said, feeling stung. She'd helped with numerous food and clothing drives in the past, and she donated to the Red Cross every year. "I've always been interested in helping other people."

Ryan smirked. "People with unlimited credit."

"I'm going to pretend you didn't say that."

"We'd better move on." Glancing at his notepad, he said, "Mrs. Edwards decided to come in today when she heard you weren't going to be in on Saturday. She's due any minute. And Jillian and I need you to look over our latest designs before we give them to Sylvia for approval."

Both jobs were ones she enjoyed. "I'll be happy to look at those sketches."

When the customer Jillian had been helping left with her new purchases, Jillian joined Tessa and Ryan on the couch. Just like old times, the three of them went over each design. Tessa made notes and offered suggestions.

By the time Mrs. Edwards arrived, Tessa felt more like her usual self.

"Tessa! I'm so glad you made it in," the older woman said, closing the door behind her.

"Thank you. Would you like some tea?"

"In a minute. Come sit down," she requested regally, leading Tessa to a love seat as she handed Ryan her fur coat and gloves. "I heard a rumor about you."

Tessa had to smile. As demanding as Mrs. Edwards was, she had a gleam in her expression that signaled mischief was always right around the corner. "You did?"

"Ryan told me you've cut your hours."

"That's true."

"What in the world is going on?"

Mrs. Edwards's hands were neatly folded on her lap, her blue eyes as perceptive as ever. Though they'd seen each other on an almost weekly basis for several years, she'd never crossed the line between work and Tessa's personal life before.

"Sylvia's not here," the older woman said, "and I've been a regular customer for almost a decade. I've purchased enough clothing from you to dress a small town. Pick a reason to be honest with me."

Tessa blinked, studying Mrs. Edwards closely. If you took away the expensive Omega necklace around her neck, the diamond earrings and the designer suit, she was just another woman. And, Tessa knew she had the potential to be a friend.

"It's kind of a long story," she hedged.

"Obviously, I have the time to listen."

"Well," Tessa began, "it all started when I took out the trash the other day." She proceeded to tell Mrs.

Edwards about everything that had gone on with Wes and his mom.

Mrs. Edwards listened closely and didn't interrupt once. Ryan and Jillian walked by a few times, but Tessa ignored their looks of interest.

"So, now this poor woman is in the hospital?"

"Yes. And I'll be taking care of Wes for at least the next week or so. Maybe even longer."

"I see." The other woman's eyes glistened. "My heart goes out to that boy. I hate to hear about children who take on so much."

"I feel for him, too. But although I'm trying to do my best, I don't know if I'm doing enough. Wes is dealing with some tough issues and some pretty difficult consequences. I'm concerned about his mom and worried that as soon as she's better, they're going to go back to living in a van." Tessa paused. "Still, I've got the feeling that I was *meant* to cross paths with Wes and his mom. Like we were meant to know each other."

"Maybe you were."

Her easy agreement was startling. "Maybe I was," she admitted softly.

"For what it's worth, I don't believe you can ever regret helping another person."

"Even if it costs me my job?"

"Let me tell you a secret, dear. You are an exceptional designer and salesperson. If you left here, I know many customers would follow you to another boutique."

Mrs. Edwards opened a small enameled box and handed her a business card. "If you need anything, please call me. I know a lot of people in this town."

"Thanks, Mrs. Edwards."

"It's June, dear."

Tessa smiled. Funny how Mrs. Edwards's use of "dear" didn't grate her…in fact, it was nice to hear.

Maybe she'd be okay after all—with or without Sylvia's support.

ONCE RYAN HAD LEFT FOR HIS class, Tessa took the time to catch up with Jillian. "How's your dog?" she asked.

"Oh, Bill's cute as can be. Todd and I walked him down to Sawyer Point and along the Ohio River yesterday."

Imagining Todd—who had the physique of a line-backer—holding the tiny puppy's leash, Tessa grinned. "I bet you three made quite a picture."

"Mmm…" Jillian said, smiling wistfully. Then she leaned forward and confided, "I think Todd's going to propose soon."

Tessa didn't bother to hold back a squeal. "Oh! That's wonderful!"

"It is! I'm so excited…and nervous."

"I can only imagine. So, are you going to say yes?"

"Of course. From the moment I first met Todd, I knew we were meant to have a future together."

Tessa blinked. "You just knew? How?"

"Everything about the two of us is right. Todd

goes to my church. We have the same values. We're two years apart in age. We both come from large families and want a lot of kids." Jillian shrugged. "He's the perfect guy for me."

The relationship sounded so perfect, *so Jillian*...so not her. "That's such exciting news," Tessa said. "You have to promise to call me the minute he pops the question."

Her friend laughed. "You know I will."

Jillian was the kind of person who knew what she wanted and made it happen. With Tessa, it was the complete opposite. At the moment, she was wanting things she'd never wanted before. Like wanting to help a boy. Wanting to make Keaton proud of her. Wanting a job with just a little more meaning.

Would she ever be planning her own wedding and speaking of being in love with absolute conviction?

She kind of doubted it, but she loved the idea of it being true.

Chapter Nine

"I'm sorry," Tessa said as soon as Keaton let her into his apartment. "I didn't mean to be so late…there was an accident on the Fort Washington Bridge." He took her coat and she rubbed her arms. "Gosh, it's cold outside. I'd be surprised if the temperature was out of the teens." She took a deep breath to keep from rambling. "Thanks for watching Wes."

"You're welcome. Come on into the kitchen."

As he led her through his living area, she took note of the serviceable couch and recliner, both in shades of brown. In the distance, she could see Wes's back through a doorway. He appeared to be playing a computer game. "Hey, Wes," she called out.

"Hi, Tessa," he replied, then turned back to face the computer.

Stepping inside Keaton's kitchen, she observed that it was also decorated in browns.

"Want a cup of coffee? I have a feeling Wes isn't going to be ready to leave anytime soon."

"I'd love one," she said, knowing that the question was a peace offering for their strained conversation two days before. Hugging her arms around her body, she added, "I hate being so cold. And I especially hate it when the air is damp but there's no snow. It just sinks into your bones."

"I know," Keaton agreed, opening a cupboard and pulling out a tin of coffee. "When I first joined the force, I always got stuck doing foot patrols on nights like this. Still, anything's better than rain. One night I had to conduct traffic for three hours in a downpour." He shook his head at the memory. "I thought I was never going to get dry."

Picturing a younger Keaton, working in the cold and rain, made her smile. "Ouch."

He chuckled. "Poor Susan would have to deal with me being crabby for hours…and my constantly running nose."

The mention of his wife's name caught Tessa off guard. Would she ever hear Susan's name without feeling surprised that Keaton had had a full life before they'd even met?

As he poured tap water into the coffee maker, she noticed a collection of bee-themed objects. A cookie jar sat on one side of the sink. A decorated wooden sign that said Bee Happy hung over the oven.

The trinkets seemed out of place in Keaton's drab, masculine apartment, and they were all covered in a fine layer of dust, making Tessa feel a little sad.

Following the direction of her gaze, Keaton shrugged. "Susan loved those country crafts. When I moved here after I sold our house, I couldn't handle getting rid of all her stuff."

"That's sweet."

He looked embarrassed. "I guess. I need to move on, put those things away, but I never seem to get around to it."

"You loved her a lot."

"Yeah, I did."

"So…what have you and Wes been doing this afternoon?"

"Guy stuff. Hot dogs. Cold soda. Computer games."

"That sounds fun."

"Yeah, we've been having a great time."

"Better than I've been having." She told him about Sylvia's reaction to her announcement that she was going to take some time off.

"Well, that sucks."

His completely male reaction made her grin. "You know, you're exactly right. It does suck. I wish things didn't always have to be so difficult."

"Seems hardly anything is easy." He pulled out a ladder-back chair from under the table. "What are you going to do?"

"Nothing." She sat down and sighed. "There's nothing I can do, really."

A small buzzer went off, signaling that the coffee was finished brewing. Keaton filled two mugs, got out the milk and a bag of sugar and placed it all in front of her, obviously remembering she needed plenty of fixings to make her coffee palatable. "You ought to learn to drink your coffee black."

She was about to offer a smart reply when Wes yelled excitedly from the other room. "Keaton! I just got to level four."

"Excellent!" Keaton said. "Watch out for the bad guys with machine guns."

Tessa chuckled. "You two really are having fun, aren't you?"

Keaton nodded, smiling. "So…we didn't get a chance to speak when you called earlier to ask me to help out with Wes. Do you want to talk about what happened at the hospital?"

"Not really." Stirring her coffee, Tessa tried to cxplain. "When I said I didn't know what to do, I was just feeling overwhelmed." Thinking back to Wes's tears in the dressing room, Tessa added, "I think we all are."

"I shouldn't have cut you off—or let you leave before I finished telling you what I'd come to say."

"Which was…"

"First of all, I found a shelter that can take Claire as soon as she's healthy enough to be released."

"That's wonderful!"

"It is. But today's news is even better. I spoke with the hospital administrator, and he's willing to hire her part-time to do custodial work."

"That's incredible."

"As soon as Claire feels better and the doctors give her their okays, she can start. Who knows? Maybe she'll even find a permanent job there."

"What you've done, what you're doing…it's great."

"Wes is a good kid. If things don't look up for him soon, that may not always be the case. I've seen good kids make some pretty bad decisions. I just want to do everything I can to prevent that."

"It makes a lot of sense to me."

He seemed pleased that they were in agreement. "Me, too."

As he sipped his coffee, Tessa took in the day's growth of beard tinting his cheeks and shadowing the lines of his cheekbones. Tufts of his honey-brown hair stuck up in places, giving him a bed-head look…making her imagine that was how he'd look first thing in the morning, tousled and relaxed.

What would those hands feel like on her skin? And how would he kiss? Somehow she didn't think he was the tender, gentle type—and that was fine—she wasn't, either.

"What are you looking at?"

"Hmm?"

"You're staring like I've got something on me. What's wrong?"

"Not a thing." Feeling her cheeks heat up, she shook her head. "I mean, nothing."

"Had to be something." Frowning, he glanced

down at his chest. "Do I have mustard on my sweater or something?"

"No. No mustard. I just...I like your sweater," she said, then laughed. "Sorry, that sounds like such a girl thing to say."

His expression relaxed. "It *is* a girl thing to say, but I can take a compliment."

"I'm impressed."

"You should be. I'm a product of a wide variety of feminine influences," he said. "I have two sisters. They were forever borrowing my flannel shirts back in high school. And Susan used to wear this sweater over some kind of legging things."

"It's nice to see a man's man like you in touch with your feminine side," she teased.

"I wouldn't go that far." As if he was surprised by the turn the conversation had taken, he coughed. "So, more coffee?"

"Sure." As she passed him her mug, her fingers brushed his accidentally. His skin was warm, calloused. So different from her own.

She snuck a glance at his mouth. Wondered what he would do if she leaned forward and brushed her lips against his.

Oh, for heaven's sake. She needed a cold shower and a reality check. The last thing in the world she should be thinking about was making love to Keaton.

But she couldn't stop picturing it.

Uncomfortable with the feelings that were

churning inside her, she glanced toward Wes. "I'd better go. I'm sure you have better things to do than hang out with Wes and me."

"This was pretty much the highlight of my evening. What do you have planned?"

Realizing that all she'd had to look forward to was a hot bath and lounging in her pajamas, she said, "Nothing."

"Do you want to play a board game or something? I have Clue and Trivial Pursuit Junior. I think Wes might like one of those."

"Sure. I haven't played either one in ages."

"Hey, Wes? You up for a game of Clue or Trivial Pursuit?"

He was in the kitchen within moments. "I'm pretty good at both. You ready to lose?"

Keaton laughed. "Never."

"Can we play Trivial Pursuit?"

"Absolutely. But I'm warning you, I don't do that chivalrous thing and let girls and kids win," Keaton said.

Tessa shared an amused glance with Wes. "We wouldn't want you to do that, would we?"

"No way. I don't do chivalrous, either," Wes piped in, his eyes shining. "I don't even let old men win."

Biting his lip to keep from smiling, Keaton said, "This is war."

"Bring it on."

Laughing, Tessa cleared off an old silk flower arrangement and took the game from Keaton. Wes helped, choosing the pink pie for her, blue for him and brown for Keaton—to go with his decor.

Keaton popped some microwave popcorn and brought out an opened bag of Oreos for them, as well. "I guess we're set," he said.

"I'll go first, since I'm the kid and all," Wes announced.

Their competitive instincts came into play from the beginning. It was obvious that none of them liked to lose.

After an hour, they declared Keaton the winner—as he triumphantly planted the brown triangle in his game piece—but not before putting up a good fight for the finish.

By this time, it was almost midnight.

"I'm exhausted," Tessa said, smiling at Wes. "How do you feel?"

"Like I could sleep for a thousand years."

"Then we'd better go on home, huh?"

Keaton stood up. After handing Wes his coat, he held Tessa's out for her. She slid her arms into it, noticing how Keaton made no attempt to move his hands away when they touched her shoulders.

"Thanks for tonight," she said softly. "It was really fun."

"I had fun, too."

She cleared her throat. "Well, we'll, uh...see you later."

"Good."

She caught Keaton's eye, and what she saw there mirrored the desire that was now snaking its way to her fingertips.

He squeezed her shoulder once, then dropped his hand.

"'Night, Keaton," Wes said, opening the door.

Keaton stepped away. "'Night."

Feeling oddly let down, Tessa forced herself to smile at Wes as they walked down the flight of stairs to her own apartment. "You okay?"

"Yep. Tonight was fun," Wes said, looking up at her.

"Yeah, it was." She unlocked her door and led him in. "I'll drop you off at the hospital in the morning so you can see your mom for a while."

"Okay." He started to head toward his room, then turned on his heel and faced her. "You know something, Tessa?"

"What?"

"Even though my mom..." He pursed his lips before trying again. "I'm glad we..."

"Met," she finished, not wanting him to have to try and verbalize everything he was feeling. "I'm glad we met, too, Wes. Really glad."

Chapter Ten

"Any more questions?" Sergeant Stark asked before dismissing roll call on Saturday morning.

Keaton glanced at Gen, who, as usual, had taken copious notes. "Need anything repeated?"

"Shut up."

In the back, Keaton's friend, Gray, spoke up. "Who's on dispatch this shift? Please tell me it's not Michele."

Stark glared. "Go down and look for yourself."

As the other officers chuckled, Gray tried to explain himself. "She was chomping gum two days ago. Every other word on the mike was garbled. I could hardly understand what she was saying."

"He has a point, Sarge," Gray's partner, Henry, interjected. "Michele's call of four-city-seven sounded more like poor-pity-heaven."

Keaton and everyone around them burst out laughing. Even Stark looked as if he was having trouble containing himself. "I hear you. And I'll make note of it." When everyone had calmed down, Stark said, "On the bulletin board is a new list of off-duties for you workaholics. Take care and call in frequently. Dismissed."

Keaton was checking his Taser when Gen, Gray and Henry approached.

"How did y'all get on today's schedule?" Gray asked. "I thought you two were off for the next couple of days."

Gen scowled. "Emerson's wife just had a baby. We're picking up his hours."

"Henry and I did that for Thompson last year. Want to meet us at Skyline when your shift's over?"

"Sure. A big bowl of their chili sounds good."

Keaton shook his head. "Count me out. I'm bushed."

"Keaton, here, has been helping out his neighbor," Gen explained. "Day and night."

Henry whistled. "The one you told us about?"

"Yeah."

"Things getting serious between the two of you?"

Keaton met Henry's gaze and saw acceptance there. It made him admit his true feelings. "Maybe."

"Maybe?" Gen asked.

Keaton cringed. Turning to Gray, he caught his eye. Gray raised an eyebrow, telling Keaton that he wasn't the only one who'd picked up on the jealous note in Genevieve's voice. He and Gen were going to have to talk about things soon.

"Phillips, Slate? You working today?" Stark called out.

"Yes, sir," Keaton replied as he followed Genevieve out the door. For once, Keaton hoped they'd be too busy to talk. He was having a hard enough time dealing with Tessa's feelings—and his feelings about her. No way was he ready to deal with two women in one day.

TESSA AND WES SPENT MOST OF Saturday at the hospital, then she ran a few errands with him that evening. On Sunday, the two of them went to Jillian's church in the morning and arrived back at the hospital mid-afternoon.

"Hey, Tessa," Wes said, when she entered his mother's room after giving them some alone time. "We were watching *The Price Is Right.* The hospital has an all-game-show channel."

Tessa glanced up at the television and saw a lively contestant eyeing a box of pasta and a bottle of detergent with expert eyes. "I love that show," she said. "But I'm horrible at guessing the prices. I wouldn't get very far."

"I like it, too. Mom would be great if she got a chance to go on. She knows the price of just about everything. Well, everything except the big items like the campers and the trucks. Right, Mom?"

Claire nodded. "I've never had much experience with those things."

She and Tessa exchanged a smile. "Are you doing better?" Tessa asked.

"I think so."

Wes shook his head. "That's not what the doctors said."

His mom frowned. "Honestly, Wes!"

"It's true, Mom," he countered. "I heard them. They said you're still real sick." He turned to Tessa. "She's going to need to keep most of the tubes in for a while. My mom has a fever and the medicine isn't helping like it should."

Claire raised an eyebrow. "I didn't know you liked to eavesdrop."

"I wasn't snooping," he retorted, studying his shoelaces. "I can't help it if they talk about all that stuff in front of me and act like I'm not there."

"Wes."

"Mom," he said, sounding completely put out.

With a defeated sigh, Claire turned to Tessa. "I guess the doctors think I should stay here a while longer. I do feel better…but I guess my body isn't cooperating very well."

Impulsively, Tessa clasped her hand. "I'm so glad you're taking care of yourself. Things will get better soon."

"I hope so."

The other woman looked drawn, ready for a nap. "Would you mind if I went ahead and took Wes with me? He and I could go to the movies, then get some dinner."

Sheer gratitude flooded Claire's expression. "Thank you."

But Wes didn't appear ready to go anywhere. "You sure, Mom? I could stay here."

"I'm sure. I'm tired."

"We could go see that new adventure movie about the family searching for treasure in the Caribbean and eat a whole tub of popcorn while we're there," Tessa said, doing her best to sound tempting.

"I don't know."

"After, we could get some pizza," she added. "What do you say?"

Wes's eyes brightened, but then turned serious again. "Is that okay, Mom?"

"I think it's an excellent idea," Claire said gently. "You can tell me all about it tomorrow night, after your first day back at school."

Panic overtaking his features, Wes groaned. "School. How am I going to get there?"

"Your mom and I talked about this yesterday. I'm going to take you," Tessa said, trying hard to sound as though she was completely prepared to handle his schedule on top of her own. "We'll come here before we go back to my place."

Wes seemed skeptical.

So did Claire. "I know we talked about you taking care of Wes for a few days, but this is turning into so much more than any of us bargained for. Are you sure you're up for it?"

There was no way she could look at either of them and say she wasn't. "Of course I am."

Moisture pooled in Claire's eyes. "I'm not going to ask why you're doing this. I just want to say thank you."

"You're welcome."

Wes still looked worried. "What should I say about you when I see my teacher?" he asked his mom. "And Tessa? And homework? I missed all last week."

Claire pursed her lips before replying. "I'll write you a note. Hey, can you find me a sheet of paper, honey? Maybe you could ask one of the nurses," she suggested.

After he'd left the room, Claire said, "I'll write a note...should I say that you'll be taking care of him for a few more days?"

Tessa knew Claire was asking far more than that. She was talking to Tessa as a mother who would do—and had done—just about anything to protect her son.

"Yes," Tessa replied, "that would be fine."

"I never meant for things to get so bad—"

"I know." Tessa placed a hand on the other woman's arm.

"Ray—my ex-husband—he made some bad decisions. At first I didn't know that he lost his job and was applying for all those credit cards. And then...I didn't know how to stop him. We owed so much, but there was always something else Wes needed." Glancing up uncomfortably, she admitted, "Ray could be violent, too. I was in a horrible situation and didn't see how things could get better. I should've just left. Now that he's gone, I seem to be paying for both of our mistakes." After a pause, she jutted out her chin in a renewed display of determination and strength. "And that's okay, but I hate that Wes has to pay for our mistakes, too."

"I won't pretend I know what you're going through. But I will say that I'm happy to help in any way I can."

Wes wandered back into the room. "I got a whole pad of paper, and a sucker!" he said, his voice triumphant.

"Did you get a sucker for me, too?" Tessa asked.

For a moment Wes looked taken aback. But then, catching her teasing grin, he said, "Sorry, you'll have to get one yourself."

"Listen to you!" Claire chided.

Tessa couldn't help but smile. Wes had sounded just like a typical kid—mischievous, with enough of a swagger to show a burgeoning independence. It gave her hope that he was starting to feel more secure again.

Claire wrote the note. "This should do the trick," she said, handing it to her son.

"We'll be back tomorrow," Tessa promised.

Tired lines were forming at the corners of Claire's eyes. Tessa guessed that she would be asleep before the two of them even made it to the parking lot.

Wes kissed his mom's cheek, then walked to the door. Tessa followed, exchanging a heartfelt glance with Claire before they exited. For a second, Tessa felt as if they were comrades.

She, who'd been so used to only thinking of herself, and Claire, who'd only been thinking of Wes.

TESSA'S CELL PHONE RANG just as they pulled up to the pizza parlor.

"Need some company?" Keaton asked.

"Sure. Wes and I just arrived at Pluto's. We're planning on eating as much pepperoni pizza as possible."

"I'm about five blocks away. Can you save two slices for me?"

She turned to Wes. "What do you think? Should we share our food with Keaton?"

"Umm..." He cocked his head, pretending to mull it over. "Okay!"

"Wes says you can come."

"I'm already on my way."

Warmth spread through her as Tessa hung up. Aside from the fact that Keaton had been an incredible help to her, she was beginning to feel that they had something in common. And then there was the attraction she couldn't deny.

She wondered if he was involved with anyone, even slightly. Most of their conversations had focused on Wes or work. She really didn't know much about him beyond the fact that Susan had been a wonderful wife and that he was obviously still mourning her death.

When Keaton walked into the restaurant a few minutes later, Wes stood up and greeted him. “We’re over here, Keaton. Tessa ordered two huge pizzas. She’s already had three slices!”

“Is that right?”

Knowing she’d turned as red as a lobster, Tessa tried to defend herself. “I happen to really enjoy a good pizza.”

“She *really* enjoys it,” Keaton said and grinned.

“Ha, ha.” Tessa glanced at him. “Keep that up and we’ll see when I invite you out for pizza again.”

Keaton picked up a slice of pizza and felt his day’s worries slide away. He was glad he’d decided to give Tessa a call. Though only a day and a half had gone by since they’d all played Trivial Pursuit, he’d found himself wondering how they were doing at the oddest times…

Yep, he’d had a good time with the kid—but even more so because of Tessa. He liked the way she wore her heart on her sleeve and lit up his room.

His apartment had never seemed as empty as it did those first few minutes after she and Wes had left. And though he had no idea where his attraction was going to lead, he knew that he wanted to see her again. As soon as possible.

He studied Tessa now and found himself charmed

by the bloom in her cheeks and the relaxed way she was interacting with Wes. He liked how she was dressed tonight, too. In the past, he'd only seen her either really dressed up or in baggy sweats. This evening, however, she was dressed casually in faded blue jeans and a temptingly soft-looking violet turtleneck. The color played off her eyes and—combined with her permanently tousled hair—made her look extremely kissable.

And that thought caught him completely by surprise.

He did want to kiss her. As she laughed at something Wes whispered to her, he imagined covering those lips with his own.

Kissing her senseless.

Hearing her whisper his name as he pulled her closer…

"Keaton? Is that all you're going to eat?"

"What?" He looked down at his half-eaten slice. Like an idiot, he'd been staring at it for a good minute.

"You okay?" Tessa asked. "Tough day?"

The question, though it was delivered teasingly, startled him. Susan used to ask him about each shift when he'd come home in the mornings. She'd draw out his worries and thoughts, knowing he wouldn't be able to rest until his mind was at ease.

"You did your best for twelve hours," she'd say, and he'd fall asleep with her comforting hand on his shoulder.

How long had it been since he'd thought about that?

"Just the usual," he finally answered, in response to Tessa's question, forcing his mind back to the present. Keaton was reluctant to go into detail about what it was like patrolling the downtown streets of Cincinnati while Wes was there. The boy had seen enough drama in his life. He didn't need the added burden of thinking about other peoples' problems.

"We've had a busy day, too," Tessa said.

"We went to the hospital and saw my mom."

Keaton glanced at Wes. Once again, he marveled at just how well he was holding up. Life had thrown him a curve lately and he'd hardly complained. "How's your mom doing?"

The boy shrugged. "Not so good."

"She said she's feeling much better," Tessa amended. "The nurse I spoke with said they're waiting for the latest test results."

"She looked tired."

Tessa ruffled Wes's hair. "She did. I know you're worried."

"We need to stay positive," Keaton said, "and leave the worrying to the folks who know what to do."

"The nurse at the station said the same thing. She said they'd worry about my mom, and that I should worry about school. That that's my job," Wes said, puffing his chest out a little.

Keaton laughed. "I've said that to my partner before. She always needs to have her hand in everything. Sometimes you just have to let other people do their part."

"Wow. You have a girl partner?"

"I do," Keaton said, "and I wouldn't call Gen a 'girl' to her face if I wanted to stay in one piece."

If anything, Wes's eyes grew wider. "I won't."

"Is it common to have a female partner?"

There was an edge to Tessa's voice that made him look at her more closely.

"I've had the same partner for three years, and there are more than a couple of male-female units. Genevieve—Gen—is great."

Wes put down his fork, a piece of lettuce still sticking to the end of it. "Is she nice?"

"Yeah, she's nice."

"What's she like? Is she like Tessa?"

The question made him smile. "Not even a little. Gen is a pretty tough cookie. I don't think I've ever seen her in a situation she couldn't handle."

Tessa frowned. "Wait a minute! I'm doing pretty good under pressure, aren't I?"

Keaton realized he'd insulted her without meaning to. "Sorry. It's just that Gen's...different. That's all."

"How?" Wes asked. "Does she carry a gun?"

"Yep. But I've never seen her draw it. She doesn't have to. Gen's the kind of woman who can do more with a few words than most people can with a whole arsenal of ammunition." Recalling the number of close calls that Gen had gotten them out of, Keaton added,

"I've seen her put everyone in their place, from petty thieves to felony suspects to our own staff sergeant."

Tessa sipped her drink. "She sounds pretty incredible."

"She is, but she can be a handful, too. She's got next to no patience and believes anything green on her plate should be removed."

Wes's bottom lip dropped so much it looked as if it was trying to leave his mouth. "I don't think I should eat anything green, either," he said.

"I'll keep that in mind." Tessa pointed to his pizza. "Finish up, 'cause we've got to get going."

"Keaton, do you think you could bring her over one day?" Wes asked.

"Sure. Next time Gen stops by my place I'll take her down to Tessa's."

"Oh my gosh. Would you look at the time?" Tessa exclaimed. "Wes, we've really got to go. You've got school tomorrow."

"Okay." He took one last bite of his pizza. Keaton found himself doing the same thing, only with much less gusto.

Something had just happened to make Tessa turn particularly chilly toward him; he wondered if she could be jealous of Genevieve. And if she was, well, that would mean she was probably interested in him the same way he was interested in her.

He wasn't sure how he felt about that.

Chapter Eleven

"This is it," Wes proclaimed somberly, as Tessa pulled into a well-marked drop-off and pick-up lane. "This is my school."

Dozens of children, all wearing snow boots, hats and thick jackets tramped around, playing with the last of the week's snow. Laughter and raucous cries echoed through the air. Suddenly, Tessa felt a little wary of leaving Wes on his own. "You sure about this?"

He turned to her in confusion. "What?"

"You going to be okay?" she asked. "Do you think you'll be all right for the whole day?" She briefly considered offering to pick him up at lunchtime.

"Yeah." He fidgeted with the straps on his backpack impatiently. "I've got to go."

The bell rang and kids scampered over the cracked sidewalks, jostling each other to get through the main doors.

"Do you want me to walk you in?"

Wes shook his head. “I’m in fifth grade. I’ll just hand the office my note and go in.”

“Sure?”

Gripping the door handle, he said, “I’m sure.”

Tessa checked her schedule again, the one she’d written down that morning over a bowl of Cap’n Crunch. “I’ll be waiting for you right here at three-ten.”

“Okay.” This time he sounded a bit exasperated, as if he was ready to go but didn’t want to be rude. She’d have to remember to tell Claire how well-mannered he was.

“If you need something, don’t forget to—”

“Call you on your cell phone. I know.” Wes patted his jeans’ pocket. “I’ve got some money and your phone number right here.”

“And…you’ll bring your homework?”

“Yup. Tessa, the second bell’s about to ring. I’ve got to go.”

Feeling oddly maternal, even though Wes’s confidence made their roles seem reversed, Tessa patted him on the shoulder. “Have a good day.”

He treated her to a bright smile then. “I will. Bye, Tessa.” Before she could say another word, he opened his door and jumped out.

She watched him walk across the large square in front of the building, nod to a few other kids, then stop to chat with a man holding a clipboard before disappearing into the old limestone building.

She missed him already.

The emotions Tessa had been experiencing all morning had caught her by surprise. Somewhere between worrying about a mysterious homeless boy and watching him walk into the school, she'd found herself really caring about Wes. Maternal feelings she hadn't known she possessed had bubbled to the surface.

"Nothing you can do now," she told herself. "He's where he needs to be." She was well aware that school was probably the one constant he'd had in his life, and she knew enough about children to know they thrived on structure. It was important for Wes to have at least one place to go where he knew what to expect.

Besides, she had plenty of things she had to do today. Like put out the latest fires at S.Y.D.

As she shifted gears and pulled away from the curb, Tessa was surprised she wasn't feeling a huge burst of relief at being on her own again. Why wasn't she excited to have her apartment to herself for a few hours?

Probably because she'd just started getting the hang of being a mom—at least a stand-in one. She thought she'd go to the store and buy a bag of Oreos or some chips for Wes, so he could have an after-school snack. Maybe she'd get him a new box of pens and pencils, too.

And a calculator. It had been forever since she'd had to think about converting fractions to decimals, which was what Wes said they'd been working on in math class. She had a feeling she was going to need all the help she could get if she was going to be checking over his homework.

When Tessa pulled into the S.Y.D. parking lot, she had to fight the urge to turn right back around. And when she saw the mess that greeted her inside, that urge tripled.

"What are all these boxes doing in the middle of the floor?" she asked Jillian, after she'd said hello. "And why are there garment bags and trash near the entrance?"

Jillian just sighed and shook her head.

Hearing the low rumble of people arguing in the back, Tessa gestured to the closed office door. "What's going on?"

"Ryan and Sylvia are in the middle of an ugly argument."

"About what?"

"You name it. The store, his pay..." Dramatically pressing her palm against her forehead, Jillian added, "It's been like this for days. I don't know how much longer I can take it."

"Ha, ha. You can handle anything."

"I don't know if that's true anymore." Waving to her notebook, Jillian continued. "Because of their feuding, I've been reduced to taking care of everything by myself. The phone's been ringing off the hook, we've gotten two deliveries and the answering machine is at capacity. I even had to cancel a date with Todd last night."

The sadness in her friend's voice brought Tessa up short. "I'm sorry."

"Me, too."

Recalling Jillian's excitement when they'd spoken last, she said, "I take it Todd hasn't proposed yet?"

"How could he? I've hardly been home. I've even had to ask the neighbor girl to help with Bill."

"I'm really sorry, Jillian. It's been crazy, trying to take care of a kid."

"I know it has. It's just that while you've been gone, everything around here has come unglued. My advice to you is either help me fix it or stay far, far away."

"How about I offer to help?"

Jillian's frustrated frown transformed into a smile. "How about I take you up on that offer?"

Tessa hugged her friend. "I'm sorry I haven't been keeping in touch like I usually do. Let's sit down and get organized before Ryan and Sylvia come back. Give me an update—don't leave out a thing."

Jillian picked up a pencil and flipped open her pink spiraled notebook. A hodgepodge of scribbled notes glared at Tessa from the page. "Maybe we'd better sit down," Tessa said.

After they'd both had a seat, Jillian began filling her in on the events of the last few days. "First of all, we had about a hundred customers on the weekend."

"That's good."

"Well, it would have been if we'd had more help."

"Was Sylvia around?"

"She was here some of the time, but not necessarily to work. She read magazines and complained. You know how she is," Jillian said, smoothing her hair away from her face like Sylvia did a dozen times a day. "Our boss avoids anything that doesn't require her immediate personal attention."

Tessa rolled her eyes. "Tell me about it."

"Then she got on Ryan's nerves by telling him to 'Wait until Tessa gets back.'"

"Of course she did," Tessa interjected dryly. "She's always made me do everything."

"Well, Ryan didn't like hearing that. Finally, at five o'clock on Saturday, Ryan blew up. He demanded she give him more responsibility. Sylvia didn't want to discuss it, so he got even madder. They both stormed out, leaving me to clean up everything." Jillian shook her head. "It was a nightmare."

"Why didn't you call me?"

"What could you have done? Told me to calm down? I assumed you were either at the hospital or busy with Wes."

Tessa rubbed her head as the muffled rants from behind the closed office door got louder. "Good Lord. Maybe I should go home."

Jillian's expression softened. "That might be a good—oh, too late."

"Tessa!" Ryan exclaimed. "You're here."

"For a little while."

"How little?"

"I have to leave a bit before three."

Ryan turned to Sylvia, who'd followed him out into the store. "Wouldn't now be a great time for us to talk about schedules and responsibilities?"

"Oh, Ryan, not right now," Sylvia snapped. "My nerves can't take any more of this."

Jillian tapped her open notebook. "What about all the things we need to order?"

"Go ahead and do it yourself. Or better yet, ask Tessa. She, at least, knows what I like."

Tessa opened and shut her mouth. *Had that been a compliment?* "Thank you, but—"

"That's not fair," Ryan interrupted. "I know what you like, I just don't always agree with you."

"I *own* this shop."

"Then you should be here more."

"Tessa's back now. Everything will be okay," Sylvia said, edging to the door.

Feeling a headache coming on, Tessa waved to Sylvia. "I'll do what I can before I go."

"I hope what you're doing for that kid is worth all the trouble you've put us through," Sylvia said, right before the door clicked shut behind her.

So much for compliments.

Jillian shook her head.

"She's driving me crazy," Ryan moaned, running his fingers through his carefully styled hair.

"That's obvious." On other days, Tessa would have taken the time to visit with Ryan and Jillian and catch up on their lives. Let them know how much she appreciated their help. But there just wasn't any time. "Ryan, we've got a few hours and no customers at the moment. Settle down and listen to me."

Tessa didn't know where she pulled her gumption from, but she delegated tasks to Jillian and Ryan and went into a kind of warp speed. Not stopping for breaks or phone calls, she threw out boxes, checked in merchandise, assisted customers and pretty much got the shop back in order.

All the while, she watched the clock. No way was she going to arrive late at Wes's school.

Finally, it was time for her to go. Tessa pulled on her coat and grabbed her purse. "Ryan, call up the university and see if there are a couple of design students who want to come in and intern. They'll need the experience, you can be in charge of them and we can use the help."

"You think Sylvia will agree?"

"I'll leave her a message, but she should. We've done it in the past."

"I'll call right away."

"Great."

"Thank you," Jillian mouthed, then, turning to the window, gasped. "Oh, look at the snow! It's really coming down."

Tessa let out a groan. On a clear day, nothing was more fun to drive than her sporty German import. But when it snowed, few cars could be worse for driving up and down the hilly streets of Cincinnati. She could almost count on the rear-wheel drive sending her into a fishtail.

"Go slow and take the interstate," Jillian said, following her train of thought. "At least it's a flat road."

"Good advice. Thanks."

Tessa had just begun to navigate her way out of the parking lot when her cell phone rang. "Tessa McGuiry."

"Hey, Tessa. It's Keaton."

She was so happy to hear from the only other person who had an inkling of what she was going through, she didn't even bother to hide her happiness at hearing from him. Even if he did have a beautiful partner who was pretty incredible. "Hi!"

"Hi, yourself. I called to see how Wes's first day went."

"I don't know. I'm on my way there now."

"You okay?"

"I will be. I had the most nightmarish couple of hours at work, and the whole time I couldn't stop worrying about Wes's first day back at school. Now the roads are nasty, and I'm going to have Wes in the car."

"Do you need a lift?"

Hearing his kind offer quieted her nerves. "I should be okay. But thanks, anyway."

"Call me if you need me."

"Thanks."

"No problem."

Remembering how they'd left each other at the pizza parlor, Tessa asked, "What are you doing later on tonight?"

"I haven't thought that far ahead. I've had a long day," he said tiredly. "I was going to go to the movies with Gen, but I went ahead and cancelled. Now all I want to do is go home and get some rest."

"Want to come over later, after you get a nap? We could have dinner. And you could help fill any gaps I have with fifth-grade math." She rolled her eyes and vowed not to analyze whether she was asking him to join her because she wanted to be with him, because she was jealous of his partner, or because she merely wanted him to help Wes with his math homework.

Somehow, she was pretty sure there was only one reason she wanted to be in Keaton's company—and it had nothing to do with homework or ten-year-old boys.

As if he'd read her mind, Keaton said, "Are you asking as an invitation or a favor?"

She grinned. It was so like him to cut to the chase like that. "Both?"

He chuckled. "I can do both. See you about six."

"Okay."

Using extreme caution, she arrived at the interstate, thankful that road crews had already been out and salted the roads. She made it to Thomas Jefferson Elementary with a full seven minutes to spare.

Joining the rest of the cars in the pickup line, she

put her car in Park and waited. The dismissal bell rang and kids slowly started trickling out.

Where was Wes?

She had to pull forward in line. Frantically, she scanned the groups of children. Checked her cell phone. Had he called without her knowing about it? Should she park and go inside?

Finally, he appeared, loaded down with books and a very full backpack. Looking far more confident than she felt, he opened the passenger door and tossed his bag onto the backseat. "Hey," he said.

She looked him over. He seemed okay—fine, in fact. So fine that the last thing he needed was to hear how worried she'd been when he hadn't exited the building right away. "Did you have a nice day?" she asked.

"Yeah. It was really busy."

"Any problems?"

"No."

She drummed her fingers on the steering wheel, reluctant to drive off in case there was anything she needed to talk to his teachers about. "Did you want—"

Puffing up his cheeks, he cut her off. "I've got sooo much homework. Mr. Baines loaded me up with history questions, and I have to practically read a whole book tonight. Tessa, are you any good at dividing mixed numbers?"

"No, but Keaton could probably help," she said,

happy that he sounded like any other kid who'd missed a few days of school—frazzled and chatty. "He's coming over for dinner later."

"Cool."

After Wes had buckled up, she admitted, "You know, I was beginning to worry about you when you didn't come out right away."

"I stayed late to talk to my teacher about my mom."

"Everything okay?"

He shrugged. "I guess. Mrs. Payne said I could have as long as I needed to make up my English." He fidgeted in his seat. "Can we go see Mom now?"

"Sure. But we'll only be able to stay for a few minutes," she said, pulling away from the curb cautiously. "The roads are only going to get worse."

"I'm starving."

Tessa grinncd. "We'll get you a snack."

"Thanks."

"You're welcome."

Wes reached for the radio tuner. "Can I turn on some music?"

"Sure."

He played with the buttons. Soon, the high-pitched whine of a teen pop star filled the sedan.

"I like this song. Do you?"

She'd never heard it. A big part of her hoped she'd never hear it again. But as she glanced his way and saw Wes mouthing along to the lyrics, Tessa knew she'd always remember this moment with happiness.

The Harlequin Reader Service® — Here's How It Works:

Accepting your 2 free books and 2 free mystery gifts places you under no obligation to buy anything. You may keep the books and gifts and return the shipping statement marked "cancel." If you do not cancel, about a month later we'll send you 4 additional books and bill you just $4.24 each in the U.S., or $4.99 each in Canada, plus 25¢ shipping & handling per book and applicable taxes if any.* That's the complete price and — compared to cover prices starting from $4.99 each in the U.S. and $5.99 each in Canada — it's quite a bargain! You may cancel at any time, but if you choose to continue, every month we'll send you 4 more books, which you may either purchase at the discount price or return to us and cancel your subscription.

*Terms and prices subject to change without notice. Sales tax applicable in N.Y. Canadian residents will be charged applicable provincial taxes and GST. All orders subject to approval. Credit or debit balances in a customer's account(s) may be offset by any other outstanding balance owed by or to the customer. Please allow 4 to 6 weeks for delivery.

If offer card is missing write to: The Harlequin Reader Service, 3010 Walden Ave., P.O. Box 1867, Buffalo, NY 14240-1867

NO POSTAGE NECESSARY IF MAILED IN THE UNITED STATES

BUSINESS REPLY MAIL

FIRST-CLASS MAIL PERMIT NO. 717-003 BUFFALO, NY

POSTAGE WILL BE PAID BY ADDRESSEE

HARLEQUIN READER SERVICE
3010 WALDEN AVE
PO BOX 1867
BUFFALO NY 14240-9952

Wes had made it through his first day back at school and was settling in. He was making this mom thing seem almost easy.

"I do like it," she said. "I mean, I think I would if I could understand the words."

"I'll turn it up," Wes offered, increasing the volume by two levels. "Better?"

The speakers were vibrating so loud, Tessa was sure they were about to blow. "Oh, yeah. I can hear it just fine, now," she said with a laugh. "But tomorrow, I'm choosing the music."

Chapter Twelve

Tuesday morning went more smoothly. Tessa drove Wes to school and watched him disappear into the mass of kids, then glanced at the clock. Eight a.m. Uneager to go back home or straight to work, she called the one person she knew she could count on. "Jillian? Did I wake you up?"

"No. Bill woke me hours ago. He makes these cute little yips around six-thirty every morning. I'm having a cup of coffee and thinking about eating another chocolate Pop-Tart. What are you doing?"

"I just dropped Wes off. Can I stop by? I don't want to go to work just yet."

"Sure, come on over. But I'm not getting out of my sweats. Remember, I don't go in today until two o'clock."

"I wouldn't dream of asking you."

Tessa hopped on I71 and drove north to Jillian's quiet, suburban neighborhood. It, and the 1950s-style ranch house she'd bought from her parents, suited her perfectly.

Jillian opened the door as soon as Tessa pulled the key out of her ignition, and Bill darted past her into the driveway. "Careful where you step, Tessa," Jillian called out as Tessa bent to play with the fuzzy black-and-white pup. "No telling what's under the snow."

As Bill licked her finger, then tried to chew on it, Tessa scooped him up in her arms, inhaling his puppy scent. "He's adorable."

"He is," her friend said with a proud smile. "Smart, too."

The three of them made their way inside. Tessa noticed a stack of photos on the coffee table, next to a trash can and some photo albums. "What are you doing?"

"Making a scrapbook. I wanted to put together an album of Todd's and my life together so far." Leaning down, she tossed Bill a stuffed dog toy.

"Your life sure is coming together, isn't it?"

"I guess so." She shrugged. "I'm really happy, Tessa."

"You deserve to be," Tessa said.

Jillian wandered into the kitchen. "Do you want some coffee? You look like you could use a pick-me-up. How's Wes?"

"Yesterday went fine." Briefly, Tessa filled Jillian in on Wes's first day back at school and the impromptu dinner at Pluto's Pizza. "What do you think I should do about Keaton?"

"Just enjoy it, Tessa."

"You don't think it's strange that there's something brewing between us? We've got so much else to deal with right now."

"Maybe your heart doesn't know that. Or care."

"Keaton's still getting over his wife."

"And…?"

Jillian was entirely too matter-of-fact. "Do you think it's possible to love again after something like that? I mean, is it possible for him to love again one day in the future? If he found the right person?"

"I don't see why not. Keaton sounds like a loving man."

That wouldn't have been how Tessa would describe him, yet she supposed it was true. "Well, it doesn't matter, anyway. This isn't the right time for either of us."

Bill nudged Jillian's leg with his black nose and she picked him up. "You've really fallen for that boy, haven't you?"

Tessa looked up at her friend. "Who are you talking about? Wes?"

Jillian nodded. "You've changed your whole life for him. That sounds like love to me."

"I do love Wes," she admitted with some surprise.

"If you can fall for a little boy so easily, and I can fall in love with a puppy in a matter of seconds, I have a feeling the idea of you and Keaton falling in love might not be as crazy as you think."

"You may have a point."

"I know I do." Cuddling Bill on her lap, Jillian cooed. "Oooh, you're so cute!"

Tessa burst out laughing as Bill demonstrated that—while very cute—he was far from potty-trained. Jillian hastily placed the puppy on the floor. "Guess you'll be getting out of those sweats, after all," Tessa quipped.

"Yeah. Hey, do you mind going outside with him?"

"Not at all. Come on, Bill, and don't even think about ruining my clothes," Tessa said, as she carried the pup outside. Obviously, Bill wasn't listening because as soon as he'd done his business, he jumped up on her, leaving dirty paw prints on her dress pants. She stooped and let him cover her face with sloppy puppy kisses.

Maybe Jillian was right about that instant love stuff.

AFTER ANOTHER CHAOTIC DAY at S.Y.D., Tessa picked up Wes from school, then drove straight to the hospital.

Still fighting a fever, Mrs. Grant seemed worn out, but happy to see her son. Her smile never wavered as Wes chatted on and on about his friends at school, what he'd had for lunch, what he'd learned in science, and what his eccentric music teacher had been wearing.

Wanting to give them some privacy, Tessa left for a while and bought a cup of coffee from the machine.

She'd mastered the process and was even getting used to the cardboard flavor of the strong brew.

When the sun began to wane, Tessa knew it was time to go home. "We'd better get going soon, Wes," she said as gently as she could. "You've got homework."

Wes looked ready, but torn between his desire to go home with her and the sense of duty he felt toward his mom. Tessa wondered if she'd been trying to do too much with him—taking him out to eat, buying him new clothes, letting him play video games with Keaton. Were her efforts only making Wes feel guilty about wanting to go back to her place? Only reminding him of how he had no real place to call home?

She shook off the thought, knowing that type of reasoning was ridiculous. Wes deserved the little treats she gave him. Besides, in the grand scheme of things it wouldn't matter what she did with Wes, anyway. He loved and missed his mother, and when she got well, he would happily go back to her, leaving Tessa all alone again.

"Tessa, can't we stay a bit longer? Maybe—"

"I think hitting the road is a good idea," Claire interrupted, her eyes betraying her exhaustion.

Wes sighed. "That means I'll have to do my homework. Mom, you wouldn't believe how much makeup work I've got."

"I believe it. But, don't you complain too much to Tessa. School is important. It's *the* most important thing."

He shook his head. "Mom—"

Claire cut him off. "The more time you spend here, the more likely you are to catch something," she said, frowning as a nurse wheeled another patient through the hallway. "Who knows what kind of germs you're picking up."

"Oh, Mom."

"It's true. Plus, I'm tired, sweetheart. It's almost time for my nap." With a smile, she brushed a finger against Wes's cheek. "I want you to go sit outside for a moment." Claire cleared her throat. "Tessa, could I speak with you for a moment, privately?"

"Sure." Fishing in her purse for another dollar, Tessa handed it to Wes. "Why don't you get a cup of hot chocolate for the road?"

"Okay." Reluctantly, he wandered out the door, the bill crumpled in his right hand.

As soon as they were alone, Claire looked at Tessa, her expression somber. "I just wanted to thank you once again, and let you know that you aren't going to have to watch my son much longer. I met with a woman from the Applegate Women's Shelter today."

"And?"

She smiled wanly. "They have two beds reserved for Wes and me, for when I get out. And Janet, my social worker, has been talking to the director here at the hospital. I guess he's a personal friend of your cop friend. He's going to start letting me work here a few hours a week when I'm feeling better."

"That's great!"

"It is. Given everything that's happened during the last eighteen months, being offered a real job feels like a miracle."

Tessa gripped Claire's hand. "I'm so happy for you."

"Me, too. I can't tell you what a relief it's going to be to start fending for myself...and to be able to have Wes with me."

Claire lifted her chin, her eyes shining as if she was hiding a secret. "I wasn't always homeless. Once upon a time, I had dreams of being a nurse. I was in community college for a whole year, learning to be a nurse assistant."

Her voice turned wistful. "I don't think I'll ever be a nurse...but I think there might be hope for me in another capacity. The reason I'm telling you this is because when I finally get better, I want to find a way to pay you back."

Claire's promise was humbling. "Let's not worry about that right now."

Claire coughed as she tried to catch her breath. "I'd rather Wes not have to go to the shelter by himself. Do you..." She swallowed hard. "Do you think you'd be able to—"

"Watch Wes until you're released from the hospital?" Tessa finished, not wanting to make Claire ask out loud. It was obvious she'd already swallowed all the pride she had.

Claire closed her eyes. "Yes."

"Of course."

"If you'd rather not—"

"I like Wes, and I like you," Tessa interjected. "We're friends now, right? Let's just keep things how they are, okay?"

Worry lines still marred Claire's brow. "When you first saw Wes in the alley and offered to help, I'm sure you never expected to take care of a ten-year-old for an extended period of time."

"Keaton, my neighbor, is helping, and Wes is easy."

Claire's eyes turned speculative. "Keaton's the cop, right?"

"Right." Tessa's cheeks heated, as she admitted to herself that there was one more reason she was in no hurry to say goodbye to Wes. His presence was providing a great opportunity to get to know her neighbor better, and to explore the chemistry they seemed to have.

Claire smiled. "Is there something going on between the two of you?"

"Of course not." *Oops, had she said that too quickly?*

With a wry grin, Claire said, "You know, I'm probably the last person who should be giving romantic advice, but I will tell you that if I've learned anything from this experience, it's that life is short. Grab ahold of what you can, when you can, and don't look back. You never know what the future might have in store for you."

"Mom, can I come in now?" Wes called from the doorway. "It's been, like, forever."

"Forever, already?" Claire replied, winking at Tessa. "Sure. Come on in, but only to give me a hug. It's time for you to go home." After wrapping her arms around Wes and hugging him close, she turned to Tessa. "Thanks, again. I'll see you soon."

Back at her apartment, Tessa got Wes started on his homework and heated up some macaroni and cheese. Then, she pulled out some lettuce and began tearing the leaves for a salad.

She stifled a yawn. Had she ever been more tired in her life? Work, the stress of driving in the snow and worrying about Wes and his mom were all taking a toll on her.

Tessa marveled at how Claire had managed to do as much as she had for Wes. Here *she* was having a tough time, and she had the luxury of a cozy apartment and a comfortable savings account.

Still, she couldn't help feeling anxious. How much longer would she be able to take care of Wes without being fired? And would Claire even get the job at the hospital?

Would Wes and his mom take off as soon as Claire got better and disappear from her life completely?

It was a relief to hear Keaton knocking on her door. She rushed to answer it. "Hey," she said.

"Hey, yourself." Keaton looked extremely huggable in a faded long-sleeved rugby shirt and khakis.

Thick socks and worn suede loafers covered his feet. "I brought a bottle of wine."

"Thank you," she said, stepping back to let him inside. "I could use a glass."

"How was your day? Better than yesterday?"

She nodded, taking the bottle from him and leading the way to the kitchen.

"How did it go at the hospital?"

"Okay. I'll tell you about it after we eat," she said, gesturing to Wes, who'd just come out of his room.

"Hi, Keaton."

Keaton clasped the boy's shoulder with one of his large hands. "How's the homework coming?"

Wes rolled his eyes. "It's neverending. But at least I don't have any math tonight."

"What? I was all set to work on some division problems."

Wes giggled. "You can help me with social studies."

"Sure thing. Go ahead and bring it over to the couch."

"Cool," Wes said, turning back around to grab his books.

"You don't mind?" Tessa asked. "You just got here."

"It's why I came, right?"

Had it been? "Oh, of course," she said, feeling her face turn red.

His eyes flickered. "Had you wanted me to stop by for any other reason?"

How could she answer that? She opened her

mouth to say something pithy, something cute, but nothing came out. Quickly, she closed it. "Maybe we should talk about that later, too?"

"I can hardly wait," he murmured, just as Wes returned.

Oh, she hoped the mac and cheese would be ready soon.

Chapter Thirteen

Two hours later, the three of them were sitting on the couch, letting their dinners digest. They all knew much more about the three branches of government than any of them ever wanted to know. Tessa was dangerously close to Keaton's outstretched arm, and Wes was dangerously close to falling asleep.

"I think it's about time to call it a night. Don't you think so, Wes?" Tessa asked, not wanting to appear too eager to send him off.

He wrinkled his nose. "No."

She glanced at the clock and wished she'd thought to ask Claire for some tips on getting Wes to go to bed. Dinner—no problem. Math and social studies—doable with some help from Keaton. But enforcing bed times, and dealing with power plays—those things she had trouble with.

She tried again. "It's nine o'clock."

"Uh-huh."

"Wednesday morning's going to come pretty early."

"I know," Wes said through a stifled yawn, but still didn't move.

Tessa glanced at Keaton for help.

"If you go to bed now without any argument, I'll come by later this week and bring my PlayStation," Keaton said.

Wes looked up. "Promise?"

"Promise," Keaton echoed, his expression leaving little doubt that his word could be counted upon.

"Okay. G'night," Wes said and scurried off to his room.

"I guess bribery can work wonders," Tessa said, a small smile tugging at the corner of her mouth.

"Hey, give the kid a break. He needs to feel in control of his life sometimes, right?"

Tessa hadn't thought about it that way, but it made sense. Wes was generally extremely agreeable—it would be wrong to expect him to constantly let her and Keaton tell him what to do, without any give and take. "That's true."

"It worked tonight. We'll see about tomorrow. I never wanted to go to bed when I was his age."

"I'm glad you came over," she said, eyeing Keaton's arm lying across the back of the couch. He looked so comfortable. Warm. How good would it feel to snuggle closer? "Thanks again."

The way he gazed at her made Tessa think that maybe—just maybe—he hadn't come over *just* to help with Wes. They watched a hospital drama on TV in silence for a few moments, the show's music mingling with muted sounds coming from down the hall. Tessa could hear Wes brushing his teeth and fussing around in his room. Finally, the sounds ceased and his light turned off.

Leaning back with a sigh, she said, "Well, I guess I can now safely say that the day is over. I'm exhausted. I don't know how real moms do this all the time."

"They do it because it's what moms do."

She caught his smile. "I guess."

"For what it's worth, I'm impressed with how well you're doing."

"I don't know about that. But, Wes seems happy to be back at school. And Claire's future looks brighter."

"See?"

"This roller-coaster ride we've been on has been pretty intense. Every time I think I've got a handle on things, I plummet into a free fall. And here we're acting like I've accomplished a lot, but it's only been a few days!"

"Come here," Keaton said softly. When she scooted closer, he reached out and rubbed her shoulder. His nimble fingers felt so good that she snuggled even nearer. "I'm sure you're doing better than you think," he murmured. "And, you've probably only got a few more days left, right?"

"Maybe." She filled him in on what Claire had shared about the Applegate Shelter and the possibility of working at the hospital.

"How do you feel about that?"

"Happy for Claire, but…I don't know," she admitted. "Taking care of Wes makes me feel good inside…I think I'm going to miss him." She let her head hang forward, so he could get at her neck. "It's just that this happened so suddenly—I feel like I wasn't even ready for it."

"I know all about that feeling."

His tone reminded her that life certainly had been unpredictable. "I'm sorry. I should be more conscientious."

"Don't worry. Life did throw some curves my way, but for the first time ever, I've been thinking about the future instead of missing the past. It's a good change." His fingers continued to massage her neck and shoulders, and she shifted to allow him better access, trying not to moan as his left hand joined his right.

"If Claire and Wes have some rocky times ahead, don't be too surprised. It's going to take a lot of hard work for them both to get back on their feet."

"Remind me of that when I start hoping for things to instantly get better."

"Anytime."

She turned to him, then. Caught her breath when she realized how close her lips were to his. How connected she felt to him.

Just how much she wanted to kiss him—and how much she wanted him to kiss her.

Keaton leaned closer, and she inhaled the tangy scent of his cologne. It sent a new wave of desire racing through her.

Tessa tilted her head up. She was so ready to taste him, to be held in his strong embrace. His lips parted, and he put a hand on her shoulder blade, bringing her closer…

Then, as if a warning siren had gone off, he pulled back. "How about I help you with the rest of the dishes?"

She blinked. "What?"

He couldn't seem to scramble off the couch quickly enough. "I think it would be a good idea if I left soon," he said, turning the faucet on in the kitchen as if the dishes were going to self-destruct, "and I'd hate to leave you with all of this."

Of course. Keaton was still obviously in love with his wife.

But there was no way she could ignore the pull that drew her to him, even to wash dishes. "You don't mind?"

"Not in the least," he said, dipping his hands into the soapy water.

Tessa reached into the sink to help—but came in contact with his hands instead of a glass. Under the water, his hands felt as compelling as they did under any other circumstances.

In fact, it was a little embarrassing to admit just how often she thought about them. About the rough calluses on the sides of his forefingers. The broad knuckles. His firm grip. The gentle way he'd massaged her shoulders just a few minutes ago.

She pulled away from the contact, then sneaked a peek at him.

"You okay?" he asked softly, making her embarrassed for thinking so much about an innocent touch.

"Sure. I'll, um, go ahead and finish up these dishes. You don't have to help."

"I know I don't...but I want to."

KEATON BLINKED. Had he really almost held Tessa's hand in the water? What was it about this woman that transformed him into a lovesick teenager?

Just being around her made him feel electrically charged. Alive and aware of everything. Colors seemed more vibrant, sounds more musical.

When had that happened?

He drained the sink, then dried his hands with a paper towel. Hoping to diffuse the tension between them, he asked, "So, what's on the agenda tomorrow?"

"Same as today. Wes has school, I'm going to go help Jillian out at S.Y.D. and attempt to keep Ryan from killing Sylvia."

He grinned at the scenario. "Are you so sure that's a good idea?"

"Honestly?"

"Of course."

She smiled then, too. "Honestly, no. They're both

driving me crazy. I'm sure I'll be counting the hours until I'm back home."

"Well, I'll be thinking of you lazing around tomorrow night. I'm working third shift. While you're sleeping, I'll be answering calls until seven in the morning."

"That sounds awful. Do you work that shift often?"

"Not really. Usually Gen and I are assigned first or second, but a couple of guys asked for some time off, so we all got switched around. No big deal."

Hearing his partner's name triggered another wave of jealousy in Tessa. A pair of glasses clinked together as she set them on the drying rack a little too quickly. One cracked. "Darn."

"Did you break one?"

No, she'd just let her emotions get the best of her. "It's only a crack." Before she could stop herself, she said, "I, uh, was hoping that we could see each other again tomorrow." *Well, there it was, out in the open.* She was obviously smitten and not afraid to admit it.

Keaton was leaning against the cupboards. His posture was relaxed, but she could tell it was all a show. "Why?" he asked, moving closer.

She swallowed. No way was she going to say any more and *really* make a fool of herself. "You're such a help with Wes."

He took another step toward her, and she felt his warm breath on her neck. "Is that the only reason?"

"Do I need another?" she asked, volleying the question back.

"Maybe."

A sassy retort died on her lips. He was close. Close enough that she could feel the heat from his body.

Ever so slowly, he reached for her wrists. Pulled her toward him. Brushed the tender skin of her hand with his thumb. "I think you have another reason," he whispered.

Oh, she wanted to be next to him. To give in to the attraction that had nothing to do with helping a child or mere friendship.

"Tessa?"

She tried to say something, she really did, but her mind kept spinning. His hands now traipsed up her arms, sending shivers in their wake.

He cupped her shoulders and turned her body toward him. Then, he splayed his long fingers across her upper back, and she slid into his embrace.

She parted her lips. Licked the bottom one. Met his smile.

And caught her breath when their mouths touched. What started out chaste quickly turned into a real no-holds-barred-hold-the-phone type of kiss. A deep honest-to-God-I-want-to-get-naked-with-you exploration.

Or so she thought until he lifted his head, and surprise replaced the hard desire she'd seen in his eyes just moments before.

She gasped as he suddenly stepped back.

Questions filled Keaton's eyes. "I…I can't say I came here meaning to do that."

"But now that we did?"

His expression shuttered, as if verbalizing the way he felt was more than he could handle.

"It's okay," she whispered. "We're both adults."

"I know. And sometimes that's the worst of it. Sometimes I wish I was back in high school, when I didn't have to worry about anything except getting the girl home on time."

"And getting to first base?"

He looked slightly affronted. "First base was a given. I was trying for at least third."

Relieved that the tension between them was broken, she teased, "I'm glad I didn't know you back then. My mother would have never let me go out with you."

"You would've begged her to let you," he retorted, laughing. "I'm going to head on upstairs. I think it's time to call it a night."

Tessa's heart sank a little as she realized that he didn't seem interested in trying to figure out what had been going on between them…or what had been about to. But, at the same time, she knew his going home right now was probably for the best. "All right, then."

"Good luck tomorrow. Stay safe."

He paused, then looked her in the eye. "Thanks."

Thanks? The word and the look he'd given her played over in her mind as he strode through the door. Thanks? For what? For kissing him senseless? For kissing him the way she'd been dreaming about for too many days?

She should be thanking him, she knew that for a fact. That kiss had been the best thing that had happened to her in a while, and it was something she knew she was going to treasure for a long time to come.

Her body, without her knowing it, had been aching for his touch, aching to be held and comforted. Taken care of.

And she had the sneaking suspicion that only Keaton Phillips would ever be able to make her feel the same way again.

Chapter Fourteen

"Penny for your thoughts," Genevieve said almost a week later from her perch on top of Keaton's desk.

Glancing up from the piles of papers and folders that seemed to be multiplying by the hour, Keaton grunted. "Are they even worth that much?"

Genevieve's eyes narrowed with new speculation, warning Keaton that she had a whole host of questions. Gen didn't know the meaning of the word subtle…or moderation.

Those were qualities that made her a fine cop. They were also qualities that made her a difficult partner. Past experience had taught him that she was about to drive him crazy with personal questions and too many open-ended comments. He opened a drawer to see if he had any Motrin left, popped one in his mouth, then glanced across the room, hoping to see Gray signaling him over.

In a last-ditch effort, Keaton gestured to the packet in his hand. "I'd better get this report done before the—"

Genevieve snatched up the folder and removed it from his view. "Not so quick." Glancing at the name on the cover, she had the nerve to roll her eyes. "And I happen to know—for your information—that this case has gone nowhere for two weeks. It can wait another five minutes."

"Gen—"

"So, what's going on?" she prodded. "What's making you reach for pain relievers and giving you that new wrinkle in your forehead? Is it work or personal?"

Before he had a chance to reply, she answered her own question. "My first instinct would be to say work, because we both know you have no personal life. Or at least you never used to." She studied him boldly head to toe.

Keaton glanced down at himself. His chinos and rumpled oxford looked okay. Comfortable. Reasonably clean. Yeah, his body could use a good run every morning. Maybe a little more weight training. But as far as he could tell, he looked the same as he always did.

Didn't he?

Frantically, he tried to come up with an excuse, any excuse to put an end to her interrogation. "First of all—"

"Trouble on the home front?"

"No." Of course, the complete opposite was true. He was in deep trouble with Tessa McGuiry.

Just thinking her name brought back memories

of kissing her. He hadn't been able to keep his hands to himself.

Though they'd seen each other several times since, there hadn't been an opportunity for privacy. Either Wes had needed help with homework or Tessa had been on the phone to Ryan, discussing work that needed to be done at S.Y.D.

Keaton missed her.

He swallowed hard as his mouth went dry. Yeah, Tessa made him hope for amnesia, or at least a really good emergency to take his mind off her. Fumbling through the stack of folders on his desk, he searched again for some work that needed to be attended to right away.

"Is your neighbor driving you crazy?" Genevieve asked, a little too loudly. "Want me to cite her for something, get her off your back?"

"Shh. She's not on my back." A startling vision popped into his head of Tessa on her back, in his bed. He shook his head to clear it, and, thankfully, the picture faded from sight.

No, she wasn't on his back at all, just on his mind. He'd gone to sleep for the past week thinking about ways he wanted to make love to Tessa. Not good.

"Don't let her rope you into nothin' you don't want to do."

He winced as Genevieve's West Virginia twang asserted itself, something that only happened when she was worried or agitated. "Thanks for the advice. Now, hand me that folder."

Reluctantly, she passed it back to him, then scooted away. "It's 5:30. Day's almost over. I know the perfect cure-all. Henry, Gray and I are going to O'Shay's for drinks and appetizers. You should join us."

Keaton forced himself to consider her offer, then questioned why he even had to make himself try. Just a few weeks ago he would have gone without hesitation, if only so he wouldn't have to face another evening by himself, with nothing but his memories of Susan for company.

But now, the idea of going out wasn't appealing. Now, he had Wes to help…and Tessa. He once again had people who needed him, a reason to get up in the morning.

Then there was the whole thing with Genevieve. His new insight into their relationship made him want to tread more carefully than usual. "Thanks, but I don't think so."

"Why not? We have tomorrow off."

"I'm not up for another happy hour. Plus, I'd better get on home."

Unable—unwilling—to let things be, Genevieve tilted her head to the side. "Why?"

"My neighbor's got her hands full." He grinned in spite of himself, thinking of last night's homework assignment. Wes had had to make some kind of flip book about crustaceans. It had been Keaton's job to comb the Internet for good photos for Wes to insert. He and Tessa had laughed and laughed about their lack of oceanographic knowledge.

Realizing Genevieve was looking at him strangely, he cleared his throat. "Wes has a lot of homework. I need to see if I can give Tessa a hand."

His partner frowned. "You didn't sign up to be Dad of the Year. I'm sure she can handle it."

"I told her I'd help. Anyway, it's fun being around Wes. Tessa and I are thinking about surprising him with a trip to Game, Set, Match on Friday."

Genevieve looked as if he'd slapped her. "This Friday? When you cancelled last Monday's date, you said we'd try again this Friday."

Date? Keaton saw her fiery expression and almost grimaced. Hurt shone in her eyes.

Choosing his words cautiously, he said, "I know we'd talked about seeing a show, but I didn't think you cared that I cancelled it when Tessa said Wes needed help with his homework. Did you?"

Genevieve shrugged. "I don't know."

"I mean, if you made last-minute plans with some other guy, I'd certainly understand."

"Other plans?" She bit her lip, as if weighing her words, then took a step toward him. "What is this night out supposed to be, really? It sounds like a date."

"It's not."

"I hope not."

"Why would you say that?"

"Because everything you've shared about Tessa tells me she's completely wrong for you. She sounds so high-maintenance and needy."

"She's not either of those things," Keaton said. "Tessa's just the kind of woman who needs someone to keep an eye on her, to make sure she's taking care of herself, because otherwise she'll only take care of everyone else. Sure, she likes clothes and expensive perfume and…"

He paused, recalling how he could've sworn he'd felt satin under her sweater when they'd kissed…and how her skin had felt so soft and smelled so good. As if she'd just showered and put on powder. And not good old drugstore powder, either.

"You just can't see beyond a good figure and pretty blue eyes," Genevieve said. She was smiling but the corners of her lips quivered.

Her words hung in the air, echoing in their section of the room. If he wasn't careful, they were going to be fodder for the next round of gossip. It was time he said something. "Gen, I'm glad we're partners."

"Me, too."

"I'd never want anything to jeopardize that."

Her gaze softened. "Me, neither."

Oh, he so did not want to do this here, in the middle of the station. But he didn't have a choice. Genevieve looked as if she was about to grab his hand. "But…I don't have those types of feelings for you."

She turned her eyes downward. "I'm not asking for you to make up some kind of feelings for me."

"Good. I need you as a partner. As a friend."

"I understand. But, do you realize that your little neighbor sounds the exact opposite of Susan?"

Her words hit him hard, taking away his breath as though she'd just punched him in the solar plexus. "She is."

"And?"

"I don't know," he admitted, his head pounding as he attempted to sort out his thoughts. "I don't want another Susan," he said quietly. His heart felt like it was shattering with that revelation. Susan was slowly fading into his past, and he was slowly stepping out of his self-induced depression. "She was terrific, and I loved her. She was beautiful, both inside and out. But she's gone."

She was never coming back. Ever.

Finally, he'd accepted that.

After a lengthy pause, Gen stepped back. "I think I'd better get going."

"See you tomorrow?"

"Sure," Genevieve said, then left the building in a hurry, leaving a few whistles and curious looks in her wake.

Great. Now he was going to get a load of grief from the rest of the squad because of...woman trouble. Popping another Motrin in his mouth, he swallowed it quickly and glared at anyone who looked as if he was about to come over with his own set of questions.

For once, he was glad to open up a file and start typing again.

"TESSA, DARLING. You're exactly the person I wanted to see."

"Hello, Mrs. Edwards," Tessa said, putting aside the pile of jackets she'd been sorting. "It's nice to see you." Stepping forward, she offered to take the lady's coat. "What may I help you with?"

Ignoring Tessa's outstretched arm, Mrs. Edwards pulled her coat more firmly around her middle. "Lunch."

"Lunch?" *Oh, Lord. Why didn't a single one of their customers eat before they came to shop?* "I'm sorry, I think all I have in the store is a can of tomato soup."

"Not here, Tessa. For heaven's sake, you didn't think I'd actually start imposing on you for meals, did you?"

"I'm sorry." Chuckling at the older lady's disgruntled expression, Tessa added, "My mind's so confused right now, I honestly don't know what to think anymore."

"Well, consider this. I'd like to take you out for lunch next Tuesday. Can you get Ryan or Jillian to cover for you?"

A week from today? "That shouldn't be a problem." Surely she'd be completely in control of things by then.

"Good. Let's go to that cute new café in Hyde Park, Illusions."

She'd heard about that place. Situated in an old turn-of-the-century house, it served seafood and pasta to people who had time to enjoy it. Ladies who lunched ate there. So did Sylvia. Tessa couldn't wait to go. "That sounds terrific."

"Noon?"

"That would be fine." Wondering if Mrs. Edwards planned to ask her to design a new gown for one of her charity galas, Tessa asked, "Would you like me to bring anything?"

"Just yourself. And a pad of paper. This is going to be a working lunch."

Tessa stifled a smile. Only Mrs. Edwards could state "working lunch" in a way that made it sound as if it was one of the ten best things to do in Cincinnati. "I'll look forward to it."

"As will I."

"May I help you with anything while you're here?"

Mrs. Edwards' eyes darted toward the office door. "Are you alone?" she whispered.

"Yes, at the moment."

"Then I'll stay and look around. However, I'm going to leave if that annoying Ryan comes in. Did you know he actually asked me for my driver's license when I handed him a check last week?"

Tessa winced. "Oh, my." Mrs. Edwards spent more money in a month at S.Y.D. than Ryan made in a year. Her husband's net worth was discreetly hinted at in the pages of *Forbes* magazine. She was the last person in the city who'd ever pass a bad check.

"And he made me wait while he answered the phone." With a disapproving frown, the lady shook her head. "Mr. Edwards was there to witness that episode."

"I'm sorry, ma'am. I'll talk with him about it as soon as he comes in."

"You might want to do that. See you on Tuesday, dear."

"Until Tuesday," Tessa murmured as Mrs. Edwards left, leaving Tessa to wonder what the lady had planned.

Chapter Fifteen

"Was there a reason you called?" Keaton asked.

"Yes," Tessa said, then took a deep breath. It was harder than she'd imagined to ask Keaton out on a date. Especially when she couldn't see his face to gauge his reaction.

Tessa suspected her tentativeness had a lot to do with the fact that, since they'd kissed, she hadn't been able to stop thinking about her new favorite neighbor.

Jillian would describe Keaton Phillips as a keeper—a guy you didn't let go of. *The right guy.*

Juggling the phone while she positioned herself more comfortably in her rocking chair, Tessa said, "I know we've been talking about doing something for Wes on Friday night. Would you still like to do that?"

"Are you asking me out, Tessa?"

His teasing, sexy tone took her by surprise. "I am. Well, Wes and I are," she corrected.

"Sounds good."

It was incredible how happy that made her feel. "Should we still go to Game, Set, Match?"

"Sure!"

Tessa chuckled. "Somehow I get the feeling you know it well."

"I do. I've spent many a night there, decompressing with my buddies over a couple of beers, jalapeño poppers and a whole lot of video games."

His enthusiasm made her grin—and made her even more eager to see him again.

He continued. "I think being in that environment is going to be really good for the kid. It's a guys' hangout. He's going to love it. We'll have some sodas, eat a bunch of fried appetizers and finish it off with burgers. It's practically paradise."

"For you, maybe," she said, laughing.

"How about I pick you two up at 6:30? That will give me time to take a quick shower after work."

An image of Keaton wet and naked flashed through Tessa's mind. "It's a date," she quipped, then leaned back her head and closed her eyes. No, it was *not* a date. Not really. They were just two people trying to do something good for a boy. She was *not* hoping to kiss him again. Not hoping to learn more about what made him tick…or how he felt about work, his family, life. Her.

Right?

"I mean, okay," she amended. Just as she realized he'd already hung up.

It's a date. Keaton was really glad Tessa couldn't see his face. If she could, she'd be questioning why he was acting like a lovesick teenager, turning five shades of red.

Like he'd never dated before.

Picking up the phone, he dialed her number quickly. "What are you going to do now? Any chance you were just going to watch TV?"

"Are you psychic or something?" she teased, then paused significantly. "Uh, what are you going to do?"

"Probably watch TV."

Her voice turned wistful, warm. "I have a Duraflame log. If we were together, you could sit here with me and watch the fire, too. Wes fell asleep an hour ago."

There it was. An invitation.

If his instincts were any good, he was pretty sure it was an invitation to more than television and prefab-log-watching. Here was his chance to test how he felt about taking their relationship to the next level.

"Or, we could just see each other tomorrow," she added, obviously uncomfortable about his lack of response.

"No."

"No?"

He coughed. The time had come. He could either take Tessa up on her offer or accept the fact that he would spend the rest of his life alone.

And he knew without a doubt that Susan would've told him he was crazy if he'd said he was going to spend the remainder of his days mourning her. Susan had known that life was for living. Lord knew she'd said that on more than one occasion when he'd come home bitter and depressed about a case.

"How about I come over?" he said.

"Really?"

He had to smile, her voice had such a pleased inflection to it. "Sitcoms are better if you watch them with someone else," he said, stating the truth. But really, it didn't matter what was on TV—they could watch the Food Network for all he cared.

"Great. I'll go get ready," she said, her voice a little breathless. "Come down and let yourself in. Don't knock…Wes is sound asleep and I don't want you to wake him. But, I'll let you do the honors and light the fire. I'll make some popcorn."

"You're going to save the log-lighting for me? Well, now I feel like a real man."

"Good. Because it's not enough that you put yourself in harm's way on a daily basis. You need to prove your prowess by lighting ready-made firewood."

"I aim to please, ma'am," Keaton said, grinning away. "See you in a few."

TRUE TO HIS WORD, KEATON appeared in Tessa's kitchen before she had a chance to push three buttons on her microwave.

Oh, he looked good.

Pointing to the wooden box near her fireplace,

she showed him where the log and lighter were. "I'll just finish up the popcorn, you go ahead."

After the corn had popped, she quickly tossed it in a bowl and joined Keaton in the living room. He glanced at her as she settled in next to him. Close enough to smell that he'd splashed aftershave on.

Close enough to want to sit even closer to him.

"I see that you got the fire started," she said inanely, liking how the flames turned purple and violet as the protective paper around the log crackled.

"I managed." He stretched his fingers out in front of him, as if he'd accomplished a great feat. Pointing to the remote, he said, "You can do the honors here. I don't care what we watch."

Her breath hitched. "Me, neither."

"Well, then." He picked up the remote and clicked a few times before landing on an old black-and-white movie. Grinning, he said, "Here we go. Cagney."

She found it interesting that Keaton liked old movies from the thirties. She would've thought he was more a *Lethal Weapon* type of guy. "You're full of surprises."

"So are you."

"I'm going to talk to Wes about Game, Set, Match tomorrow morning."

"Good."

"I..." She tried to think of something, anything, to say besides what was on her mind—that he looked awfully good in that old chambray shirt and jeans.

That she noticed his jaw and cheeks were

unshaven but she didn't mind. That there was something about a day's growth of beard she found incredibly appealing…

He met her gaze. "Come here, Tessa."

She nestled closer to him and he ran a hand down her arm, then down her back. His fingers were slow, searching for something. Suddenly, he shook his head and chuckled as if he had a secret joke.

"What?" she asked.

"Nothing."

"Come on, what?"

"It's nothing," he replied, with a hint of embarrassment. "It's just—I've been fantasizing about satin." Shaking his head again, he said, "The other day, when we kissed and I, uh, had my hand under your sweater, you had on some kind of satiny camisole."

"You've been thinking about my lingerie?"

He turned away, but not before Tessa caught a red stain on his cheeks. When he turned back, his expression was amused—and a little bit wicked. "It's just that Susan always wore the plain cotton stuff. There was nothing wrong with it, but…" His voice drifted off. "Never mind. Obviously I need to get out more."

Well. That was interesting. "Anything else you'd like to tell me about?"

His eyes flashed, as if there were many things he was tempted to tell her. Instead, he laughed softly. "No. Can we just forget I mentioned it?"

"I don't know if that's possible," she countered,

loving the thought that he'd been thinking about her. Loving the thought that she did something completely different than his wife, and he approved.

As she'd hoped, Keaton looked even more embarrassed. "Honestly, Tessa—" he began, but stopped as he realized what she was doing.

Smiling seductively, she unbuttoned the top three buttons of her cream-colored cardigan, then slowly slid the right section off her shoulder…just enough to reveal a satiny lavender bra strap and the edge of a lacy cup. "Is this what you were curious about?"

She felt branded by his gaze as his eyes widened and he took in every inch of her exposed body. She leaned forward and the sweater slid another two inches off her shoulder.

Groaning, Keaton reached out and traced the line of her bra strap.

She blinked twice. He looked up from the clandestine path his finger was making and met her eyes. He smiled a crooked grin, as if he was warring with a thousand mixed emotions. "I pictured it differently," he said.

What did that mean? Pictured it differently, how? Better? Sexier? Worse?

Keaton pulled her close and kissed her before she could voice a word of indignation.

And then, there she was again, lost in the comfort of his arms. Best of all, she loved the way he kissed her as if it was the most natural thing in the world.

There was no awkwardness, no sign that he was about to regret their intimacy. No, Keaton Phillips kissed with confidence. And pleasure.

"This is getting to be quite a habit," Tessa said a little shakily.

"A good one, I think." He pressed one of his fingers to the spot where her sweater gaped open, between her breasts. "But it's not the right time." With a sigh, he moved away. "Better button up, sweetheart."

Button up? Of course, what had she been thinking with Wes just down the hall? "Do you still want to watch a movie?" she asked, doing up her buttons, her face flushed.

"Sure. Turn up Cagney. This is the good part."

Keaton stayed another hour. Another very chaste hour, in which Tessa remained hyperaware of his every movement. At the door, when they finally said good-night, he kissed her one last time, letting her know without words that he'd rather have done so much more…if he hadn't been a man of principle.

She went to bed, reliving their kisses, remembering how it had felt to bare that small bit of skin to him, and savoring his look of appreciation.

Daring to hope she'd be in his arms again… very soon.

Chapter Sixteen

As Tessa walked down the hall toward Wes's room the next morning, she smiled to herself. Never before had she thought of herself as being domestic or motherly—not even remotely. But now all she wanted to do was bake cookies and think of ways to make Wes happy.

Knocking softly on his door before cracking it open, she called out, "Wes?"

He sleepily opened one eye under his fringe of messy blond bangs. "Yeah?"

"It's time to get up. Can I come in for a moment?"

He shifted himself onto his elbows. "Yeah, sure."

Tessa crossed the floor to his bed, noting the pile of clothes on the floor, the school books on a chair and the quilt bunched up around Wes's feet. The room was warm and toasty…and smelled unmistakably of boy. It brought back memories of her brother James's room, from when they were young.

Perching on the edge of the mattress, she asked Wes, "Did you sleep okay?"

He yawned and nodded, treating her to a smile. It warmed her heart and made her spill her secret sooner than she'd intended. "I was going to wait until we were having our cereal but…I've got a surprise for you."

Wariness, instead of excitement, crossed his features. As if to shield himself, Wes pulled his flannel sheet up a little higher. "What is it?"

Belatedly, Tessa realized Wes had had enough surprises for a lifetime. "This is a good one, I promise." She continued quickly. "Keaton and I thought the three of us would go somewhere fun on Friday night."

"Where?"

"Game, Set, Match. Have you heard of it?"

He gave her a look that said he would've had to be from another planet not to know it. "That place is supposed to be really expensive. Why would we go there?"

Kind of disappointed that he wasn't jumping up and down on the bed from excitement, she said, "We thought you would like it there. I hear they've got all kinds of arcade games."

"Is it your birthday?"

"No." She looked at him, realizing she'd never asked him when his birthday was. "Is it yours?"

"Nope. Mine's in July."

"I'll remember that. No, we're just going for fun."

Wes still appeared skeptical.

"We've got lots of things to celebrate, too." She rushed on. "You've made it through almost two weeks of school since you've been here."

"That's not a big deal."

"How about we celebrate the fact that your mom's doing a whole lot better?"

He stared at her for a few moments before finally giving her a real look of pleasure. "Cool."

She was so relieved, she was sure Wes noticed her shoulders sag. "I think it sounds cool, too. Well, we'd better get a move on or you're going to be late, and we can't have that."

"No, we can't, can we?" Wes joked.

His kidding raised her spirits. As she walked out of the room, Tessa reflected on the fact that she, too, had a lot to celebrate. No matter what else was happening in their lives, she and Wes were forming a friendship. One that was definitely cool.

"I LOVE THIS PLACE," Wes said to Keaton on Friday night, his eyes shining as he folded another wad of tickets and stuffed them into a large paper cup.

Keaton grinned. Obviously, Tessa's idea of coming to Game, Set, Match had been a good one. They'd only been there for twenty minutes, but already Wes had toured the entire facility and made a beeline for his favorite games.

"I love it, too. You'll score a lot of points with Tessa if you tell her how much fun you're having when she gets back from the ladies' room. She's been really excited about bringing you here."

"You think she's having fun, too?"

"I *know* she is," Keaton replied, thinking how he and Tessa had been perfectly content to simply watch Wes have a good time. Although Keaton was no stranger to the restaurant, he'd only ever gone with his buddies. Playing the games had been secondary to drinking a couple of beers and simply letting off steam. Seeing the place through the boy's eyes made him look at it in a whole new light.

Wes took a big gulp of root beer before gesturing to another section of games. "This is so awesome. I've already played Skee-Ball and Mole Hole. I think I'll go to the motorcycle rides now." Eyes darting from one flashing arcade game to the next, Wes said, "I'm going to have, like, a hundred gazillion tickets."

"You can use whatever is on the game card, but that's it," Keaton warned, gesturing to the credit-card in Wes's hand. "The balance on it goes fast, believe me."

Wes sighed. "I know."

"Have you collected lots of tickets here in the past?" Tessa asked, making it obvious that she'd heard the tail end of their conversation.

Keaton pretended to look shocked. "Of course. Why else did you think I came?"

Before she could answer, Wes announced, "I'm going over to the motorcycle rides," and darted off.

Tessa appeared worried for a second but then visibly relaxed when she saw that the ride was well within her line of vision.

She looked so cute and maternal that Keaton squeezed her shoulder. "You doing okay?"

She held up her beer and cast him a distinctly unmaternal smile. "Definitely. The drink tastes good, and it's great to see Wes so happy, especially after his visit with his mom."

"What happened there?"

After checking to make sure Wes was all right, she led the way back over to their booth, where their server had brought a basket of chips. "Things were pretty intense today," she admitted, picking up a French fry.

"What happened?"

"Claire's ready to leave the hospital. She finally told Wes about the Applegate Women's Shelter."

Just thinking about Wes being uprooted again made Keaton grimace. "That must've been tough."

"Yeah. I could tell Claire was nervous, and I think that made Wes uptight, too. They hardly looked at each other. I felt so bad for both of them." Linking her fingers through his, she added, "They're having to deal with so many changes. I didn't know what to say."

Keaton smiled. "I don't think anyone expects you to solve all their problems, Tessa," he said gently, rubbing his thumb over the top of one of her delicate knuckles. "You've already done a lot for both of them."

She blinked. "Oh, I know that. And, I know I shouldn't expect to change their lives. I mean, I don't have any experience with all this. I just..." Her voice drifted off and she shrugged. "I just feel bad for both of them."

"The shelter is a step up from living in a van."

"I guess. Janet thinks the homelike structure will be great for them. Claire also talked about her new job at the hospital. She's excited about starting on Monday."

"I bet."

"I hope she doesn't get sick again."

"If she does, she'll be in a better place to get help."

"That's true." Sighing, she said, "I tried to tell Wes that it was terrific his mom was doing so well."

Keaton squeezed her hand. "It is."

"Before I know it, he'll be back with her. Where he belongs."

She looked so wistful, Keaton felt like hugging her. "Yep."

"I'm sorry I brought this up, but it's been weighing on my mind all evening."

"Don't apologize. I wanted to hear about your day. We're friends, Tessa. Remember?"

The look she gave him was so grateful, so warm and appreciative, Keaton had to glance away. Even though he was the one who'd said it, he felt that they were far more than friends. He knew his feelings were much more complex than that.

Abruptly, Tessa withdrew her hand from his. The break in contact made him feel sad. He tried to think of something to say to disguise his disappointment. "Wes is having fun."

"Yeah. I'm really glad we came."

"Me, too." He nodded toward a pinball machine. "Want to give it a try?"

Standing up, she said, "Why not? I have a couple more bucks on my card."

"I'll play you, then. I've got my eye on a ball cap," Keaton said, standing up.

"Hey, I do, too!"

He laughed. He'd pay money to see Tessa run around town with a Game, Set, Match cap perched on her head.

Frantically, she began pushing knobs, laughing when bells and whistles rang shrilly.

Her eyes sparkled, and her sassy, short hair was messier than usual. She wore a snug black turtle-neck, low-cut jeans and black boots with a good three-inch heel.

Her outfit wasn't that different from what most other women were wearing, but on Tessa, it looked sexy. She had the type of figure that caught his eye and held on to it. And now that he had an idea about what was under that turtleneck, he was eager to see it again.

There was no denying it, he wanted her.

"Keaton!" she called out, pointing to the long

stream of tickets shooting out of the machine. "I think I'm going to have enough to buy two hats."

"Great! We'll wear them around town."

"At least in the apartment complex."

"Careful, our landlady's going to say we're a couple."

Tessa's eyes widened, but she didn't say anything, giving Keaton hope that they were on the right track. He hoped she was as okay with their relationship progressing as he was.

"Keaton!" an altogether different voice called out. "What are you doing here?"

Turning, Keaton came face-to-face with Gray, Henry and Genevieve. All three had beer bottles in their hands and appraising expressions on their faces. When he caught Gen's eye, she turned away, obviously embarrassed that he knew exactly why she'd shown up—to check up on him.

He turned to Tessa. She was holding her container of tickets and smiling at his friends. Keaton noticed Gray and Henry were having no trouble smiling back. Yeah, that whole snug turtleneck, low-rise jeans thing did look awfully good on her. Too good.

Suddenly, he found himself wishing she'd worn an oversize sweater that went to her knees.

"Hey, guys," he said, not even pretending to sound happy to see them.

All three of them nodded at him, and Gray extended his hand to Tessa. "Hi. I'm Gray Peterson."

"Tessa McGuiry. It's nice to meet you," she replied, shaking Henry's hand next. "We met briefly at the hospital," she said to Genevieve. "All of you work with Keaton, right?"

"We do," Gen replied.

Henry grinned. "Keaton struck gold when he met you…you've got to be, like, his perfect date. He loves this place!"

A pretty pink glow filled her cheeks. "I'm having fun, too."

"I bet," Genevieve said.

"Actually, we're only here because of the boy Tessa's taking care of."

Tessa's eyes suddenly grew wide, and she turned and gripped his arm. "Oh my gosh, Keaton. I forgot to see where Wes went after the motorcycle ride. I'd better go find him. Excuse me," she said.

His friends made no secret of checking out her figure as she passed by.

Henry whistled. "She's a looker, K. What's she doing with you?"

Gray laughed. "She's obviously got no taste. We'll have to dispel any notions she has about you being charming or fun to be with."

"Hey—"

Before Keaton could finish, Genevieve interrupted him. "She's only his neighbor. They're doing good deeds together."

Keaton couldn't be sure if Genevieve was trying

to protect him from any unwelcome gossip, or if she simply didn't want to believe that there could be more to his relationship with Tessa.

But he wanted to make sure there were no misunderstandings, now that he and Tessa had come this far. "The truth is," he said, "that's how it started out, but it's turned into something more. She's pretty special."

"No argument there," Henry murmured.

Keaton was about to give him a piece of his mind when he caught Henry's gaze. The look in his buddy's eyes said that he was glad for Keaton and that he knew exactly what a long, difficult time he'd had getting over Susan's death.

"That's pretty cool that you're helping the kid out," Gray said.

"Tessa's doing most of it."

"She's practically a saint," Genevieve quipped a little too brightly.

And that was—of course—when Tessa appeared behind her with Wes. By the expression on her face, everyone knew she'd heard Genevieve's sarcastic remark.

"Damn," Keaton muttered, as he stepped closer to Tessa's side, ready to do his best to diffuse the situation.

But Tessa merely touched Wes's shoulder as she began introductions. "Gray, Henry, Genevieve, this is Wes Grant. Wes, all these people are police officers with Keaton. Isn't that neat?"

Tessa's voice held a healthy dose of respect for Keaton and his friends. In turn, Keaton felt his respect for Tessa rise. It was a sign of her integrity to not get ruffled by Gen's comments and focus only on Wes's happiness.

Wes's eyes widened. Keaton's friends, being the good cops they were, slapped him on the back, checked out his stash of tickets and offered to go buy him another root beer. Tessa nodded her consent, and Wes went off with the three of them.

"I'm sorry about that," Keaton said when they were alone again.

"You've nothing to be sorry for."

There was a new wariness in Tessa's eyes, however. "Genevieve, she's got some issues," Keaton began, taking a fortifying sip of his Coors. "She doesn't always think before she speaks. I'm sure she didn't mean anything by what she said."

Tessa's lips curved into a half-smile. "I may be pretty clueless when it comes to homeless kids and crime on the streets, but I know a jealous woman when I see one. She's staked her claim on you...and doesn't want to let you go without a fight."

"There's never been anything between Gen and me," Keaton rushed to explain. "We became partners right before Susan died and worked well together. After the accident, I probably confided in her more than I should have. We started going out to lunch together. Lunch turned into dinner. Eventually, we started catching a movie once a week.

"I guess Gen hoped it would lead to something more." Feeling his cheeks heat up, Keaton winced. "God, I sound so full of myself. What I meant was—"

"That you're attractive, smart and fun to be around?" Tessa interrupted, her eyes flickering with amusement. "I can see how Genevieve might think that."

"You think I'm fun to be around?" Keaton asked teasingly.

Tessa laughed. "I do now—even though I can't tell you how many times I actively tried to avoid you in the parking lot before this whole thing with Wes. I was sure you had to be the surliest, least fun person in Cincinnati."

"I didn't think too highly of you, either. You were so self-important when you complained to me about lifting weights."

"Hey, I'd wake up every morning at five to loud clanging above my head."

"You could've been nicer—"

"You could have been more considerate." Tessa took a step toward him and murmured, "We're not going to argue anymore tonight, are we? Because I was having a really nice time."

Keaton reached out and caressed her back, loving the feel of that turtleneck under his hand.

"Don't you think it's kind of ironic that now that

I'm dying to be alone with you, I can't be?" Tessa whispered.

His mouth felt like cotton. "I thought I was the only one thinking that."

"Believe me, you're not." She leaned forward, encouraging him to slide his hand across the planes of her back. Beneath the thin material of her sweater, he could feel the outline of her shoulder blades, the curve of her spine.

"Where do you suggest we go from here?" he asked, his voice sounding hoarse to his own ears.

"Janet suggested I keep Wes for a little while until Claire gets settled into the shelter. Wes spends the majority of time at school, and Claire will be able to spend a few days learning her job before she has to worry about Wes."

"You're okay with that?"

"Definitely. I'm finally feeling as though Wes and I have a routine." Lifting her eyes to meet Keaton's gaze, she added, "Wes is going to stay at the shelter with Claire this weekend. Maybe that could be our chance."

For what? he almost asked. A night spent together in her bed?

A night out on the town, when he could take her out and flirt with her over a good dinner? He realized then that he'd be happy to do anything as long as they were together. "That sounds good," he said.

She was too tempting not to seal the deal with a kiss. Bending toward her, he gently brushed her lips with his.

"Whoa," a voice said from behind them. "Sorry."

As Tessa stepped back in surprise, Keaton ran a hand over his face. "Hi, Gray."

"Sorry to interrupt. I just wanted to let you guys know that we all chipped in and bought Wes a few more dollars on his card."

"That wasn't necessary," Tessa protested.

"It was our pleasure. He's having a good time."

"I'm going to go check up on him," Tessa said, then glanced at her watch. "It's going on eight o'clock. Probably wouldn't be a bad idea to think about leaving soon."

"I'm fine with that," Keaton said.

He was fine with a lot of things, suddenly.

Most of all with Tessa. *Especially* with Tessa.

Chapter Seventeen

Tuesday morning dawned bright. All the remaining snow had disappeared and been replaced by clear blue skies. The crisp fall day made Tessa smile…and so did the realization that Thanksgiving was only a little more than four weeks away. Before she knew it, she'd be making the trek up to Columbus to visit her family. Her mother would roast the biggest turkey she could fit in the oven, her dad would try to pretend he cared who won the football games and she would sit on the couch with James and reminisce about old times.

For one day, time would turn back, reminding her of how things used to be.

But something told her that chances were good she'd be spending the day wishing for one special man to be by her side. Someone who'd enjoy her mother's cooking and would actually care about the Cowboys' defensive line. A guy who could joke with James and help her set the table, then hang out on the couch with the best of them. *Keaton.*

Maybe she should ask him to go with her...

Casting another glance at the alarm clock, Tessa forced herself to climb out of bed. She had to wake Wes in a few minutes.

She now felt almost adequate in the morning-routine department. With practiced efficiency, Tessa woke up Wes, fed him breakfast, then shuttled him off to school. Next, she drove to S.Y.D., where she spent a good hour calming Sylvia down from her latest crisis.

At noon, she met with Mrs. Edwards at Illusions. While she was nibbling on the most exquisite trio of sandwiches, Mrs. Edwards pulled a pamphlet out of her large purse.

"What's this?"

The elderly lady tapped two fingernails on the table. "It's Designs for Success."

Tessa pushed her plate to the side and opened the brochure. Designs for Success was an organization that worked with women, who, for a variety of reasons, were entering the workforce late in life. It helped them prepare for interviews and build their self-esteem. Additionally, the women were provided with business attire. Some were given an interview suit; others were given two or three outfits to wear after they were hired.

Tessa was immediately intrigued. "I've never heard of this organization before."

"That's because there isn't a branch in Cincinnati...but there should be. They just need someone willing and qualified to step up and manage things.

Someone who's good with people, knows the clothing industry and what it takes to run a reputable company. You have all those qualities."

"Thank you, but..." Tessa didn't quite know how to respond. "I'm not sure if I'm the right person." Realizing how that sounded, she rephrased what she'd said. "I mean, I don't think I could manage both Designs for Success and S.Y.D."

"Of course you couldn't do both," Mrs. Edwards agreed. "Designs for Success is going to need someone full-time to head it up."

Tessa felt as if they were talking in circles. "Well, hmm..."

"Ever since you told me about that boy and his mother, I've thought about what a perfect fit you would be for Designs for Success. Please think about the difference you could make in other women's lives." She reached out and touched Tessa's hand. "Think about the difference you could make in your own."

The words stilled Tessa's heart. But before she could conjure a reply, Mrs. Edwards continued. "Not everyone could do this, Tessa. But *you* could. You've got everything you need to make this venture successful. My friends and I will be happy to back you financially, but most of all, you have talent. Talent to help women feel good about themselves." Lowering her voice, she added, "And you have the heart to make it work."

The older woman's confidence in her and the new

opportunity that had suddenly presented itself had Tessa's mind spinning.

"Mrs. Edwards, I—"

"Tessa, do it because you can."

Stunned, Tessa stared at the older woman, and let the repercussions slide over her. Because she could. *Because I can.* Isn't that what she'd told Claire?

"Just promise me you'll think about it."

Slipping the brochure into her purse, Tessa nodded. "I will. Thank you."

"You're very welcome, dear. Now, we must try the iced lemon cheesecake. I've heard it's positively divine."

"YOU'RE GOING TO love Bill," Tessa said to Wes as they walked up the neatly shoveled path to Jillian's door. "He's only ten weeks old."

Wes studied Jillian's house warily. "She won't mind that we're coming over?"

"Not at all. She's anxious to meet you."

"What did you tell her about me?"

Confused, Tessa turned to look at him before she rang the doorbell. His posture was stiff and he seemed troubled. Even though she knew Jillian would wonder what was going on, Tessa gestured to the front stoop. "Want to sit down for a minute?" Wes took a seat and she settled next to him. "Wes, I think of you as a friend—"

"Yeah, right."

His bitter comment caught her by surprise. "I do. I'm glad I met you. What do you think of me as?"

Wes lifted his head slowly, his brown eyes full of emotion. "You're the person who saved my mom."

Tessa's heart felt as if it had stopped. "Oh, no, I'm not. *You* are. *You* came and got me, remember?"

"Mom says we owe you so much. You bought me clothes and took me out to dinner."

"I wanted to do those things."

Shaking his head, he continued. "You've had to watch me and take me places when you probably didn't want to."

"I've *always* wanted to," she said, realizing how very true her words were. "Ever since we met in the alley, I've wanted to do everything I can for you."

"Because I'm poor."

"No," she said firmly. "I didn't do any of those things because you're poor or because I had to. I did them because I like your company, Wes. I enjoy doing homework with you. I have fun playing Trivial Pursuit and Clue." She wrapped an arm around his shoulders. "I love how you'd eat pizza every night with me if we could. I love being your friend. But Wes, most of all...*I love you.*"

A ragged sigh erupted from him, and he flung his arms around her. Fighting off tears, Tessa hugged him close.

When he pulled away, Wes pointed to the window next to Jillian's door. "Look!"

Bill, all six pounds of him, had his nose pressed against the glass and was staring at Wes like he was his new best friend. Tessa laughed. "I told you he was adorable. You ready to play with him?"

"I've never seen a puppy so small." When Bill placed both front paws on the windowpane, Wes cried, "Look, Tessa, he's trying to get to us!"

Giving Wes a hand up, Tessa said, "Let's not make him wait another minute. Ring the doorbell, would you?"

She couldn't hide her smile when Jillian opened the door instantly and Wes walked right inside. "I'm Wes," he said. "Tessa's friend."

Picking up a squirming Bill and handing him to Wes, Jillian said, "Hi, Wes. I'm Jillian, and this is Bill. We're very glad to meet you."

Wes let out a boyish giggle as Bill licked his nose.

As Wes followed Jillian into the living room, Tessa paused for a moment, her heart full. She really did love this little boy. She loved making him happy.

In many ways, she needed him in her life as much as he had needed her.

Chapter Eighteen

Throughout the rest of the week, Tessa found she was having a hard time thinking about anything besides her meeting with Mrs. Edwards. The opportunity to start her very own business. To put her skills to work for something worthwhile.

To help people like Claire.

All of it sounded so right it was scary. Repeatedly, she weighed the pros and cons. On the one hand, she wouldn't have to work for Sylvia anymore, but if she failed, she'd be the one to take all the blame and accept the responsibility.

And then there was the fact that for years, she'd focused on one day opening a boutique to showcase her own designs. And if she was being completely honest, she had to admit she'd been looking forward to reaping some of the rewards that Sylvia had earned. A part of her really did long to see her name in magazines and fashion quarterlies, to be able to afford trips to London and Paris…

Thank goodness Tessa had some time to mull it over, because she had plenty of other things to deal with first. Currently, it was taking Wes to the Grants' new home, the Applegate Women's Shelter.

As she drove along Columbia Parkway, Tessa glanced Wes's way. "You doing all right?" The boy seemed quieter than usual, more introspective.

"Sure."

"Do you want to talk about anything? I bet you've got a lot of questions."

Wes shrugged. "I'll be okay. I'm just wondering what it's going to be like."

"From what your mom said, this shelter sounds like a good place to start. You two will have your own room, and you'll be able to live there for a few weeks or months until your mom gets back on her feet."

"Do you think one day she'll have a permanent job?"

"I hope so."

"She said she wants to keep working at the hospital, get a job working with patients. She likes helping people."

"Your mother's got a good heart. I bet she'd be great with patients."

Glancing out the window, he added, "If she got a real job, things could be different."

Tessa's heart went out to Wes. All along, he'd seemed far too mature for his age, too willing to take everything in stride, always putting his needs and wants behind what was best for his mom. At the same time, Tessa couldn't forget the desperation she'd seen in his eyes that first night they'd sat together in the hospital waiting room. The whole experience—the homelessness, going to live with Tessa, missing days of school and having to catch up—had been out of his control. It had to be taking its toll.

Cautiously, she said, "When you and your mom get settled, maybe you could concentrate on just being a kid again."

He wrinkled his nose. "I *am* a kid."

"I know…but you've had to make some pretty grown-up decisions."

"Like ask you for help?"

"Like that," she said, recalling how scared they'd all been that night Tessa had followed Wes to his mother's van.

"Mom and me, we stick together."

"She's lucky to have you."

"I'm lucky, too."

Afraid if she said anything more about that night, she'd get all mushy, Tessa pointed to the set of directions Wes held. "Where to now?"

"Um, turn right after two blocks."

"Gotcha."

A few minutes later, they pulled up to a neatly kept redbrick house at the end of a cul-de-sac. A small, artsy sign out front said, Applegate House.

"Here we are. This looks nice."

"Yeah," Wes said, sounding a little surprised. "It does."

Tessa parallel-parked a couple of houses down. "You ready?"

Wes nodded. Together, they tramped down the sidewalk. Wes rang the bell, and within seconds, Claire opened the door.

She looked completely different from the sickly woman at the hospital. Dressed in jeans and a fleece top, she appeared much younger. Her hair was pulled back in a simple ponytail, and though she wore no makeup, Claire looked as if she'd been made over. Gone were the dark circles and worry lines surrounding her brown eyes. She seemed refreshed—and full of hope.

As soon as Wes stepped into the house, Claire reached out and hugged him tight. "Look at you," she murmured, smiling through a sheen of tears.

Then, lifting her head, she said, "Hi, Tessa. Thanks for bringing Wes over."

"You're welcome. Hey, congratulations! What a week you've had! I'm so glad you're feeling better."

"Thanks. Me, too. Want to sit down for a few minutes?"

Claire led the way to a large den, decorated with mismatched but comfortable furniture. Wes seemed to be taking it all in. "There's a TV room right through that doorway, if you want to go check it out," his mom offered.

Wes nodded and wandered off, leaving Tessa and Claire alone.

"I'm really happy for you," Tessa said.

"I feel great. I'm working twenty hours a week at the hospital, mopping floors and doing laundry. It's hard work, but I like it."

"Wes told me you enjoy working there."

"I do. One day I'd love to get a job working with patients." Shrugging, she said, "I don't know if that'll ever happen, but Janet told me they have job openings there all the time. Maybe one day I'll get my chance."

"I hope you do." Tessa patted the couch. "This place is cute."

"I like it. Oh, it's nothing fancy, but compared to what Wes and I have been through, it's a big step forward."

"He's missed you, Claire."

Relief filled her expression. "Thanks for saying that. I was worried he might be angry with me."

"That couldn't be further from the truth."

Claire clasped her hands in front of her. "I can't tell you how bad I feel about what he's had to deal with."

"He loves you." Wes entered the room then, and Tessa stood. "I bet you two would like to spend some time together without me. When should I pick up Wes on Monday?"

"How about eight?"

"Sure."

Eyes shining, Claire turned toward Wes, "Guess

what we're going to do today? We're going to a fall festival outside the city! There are going to be hayrides and hot cider and rows and rows of pumpkins."

Tessa looked at Wes and grinned. He was trying to act like he was too cool for the excursion, but she had no doubt that inside, he was eager to go.

Claire ruffled her son's hair. "We're going to have so much fun. Don't even try to pretend like you don't want to go on a hayride."

"I bet they'll have a corn maze," Tessa added. "Those can be scary. When I was twelve, I got lost in one for almost an hour."

"Can we go in the corn maze, Mom?"

"Of course," Claire laughed.

"I can't wait to hear all about it on Monday," Tessa said, pausing in front of the door. Catching Wes's eye, she tried to convey all of her feelings to him. This was going to be her first night apart from him in almost four weeks, and she was going to miss him.

As if he felt the same pull, Wes stepped forward, then stopped suddenly.

It was an awkward moment. No way did Tessa want her relationship with Wes to interfere with the relationship between him and his mom. Bending down, she gave him a quick, friendly hug. "Bye."

"Bye, Tessa."

On her way out the front door, she heard him say to Claire, "Can I see your room?"

"Of course. It's yours, too, you know."

An overwhelming feeling that everything was going to be okay washed over Tessa. And as she strode down the street to her car, she couldn't stop smiling.

"I HOPE WES AND CLAIRE ARE doing all right," Tessa said to Keaton for what was easily the twentieth time. Her feeling that everything was going to be okay hadn't lasted very long.

Soon after she'd dropped off Wes, she'd given in to temptation and called Keaton at work. He'd just come off his shift and his eagerness to see her had matched her own. Like a kid counting down to Christmas, she could hardly wait to spend some time with him.

But now that they were alone, Tessa couldn't help thinking about Wes and Claire and wondering how they were doing. She suspected that she felt the way most real mothers would.

That caught her up short. Poor Claire! Tessa could only imagine how much she'd worried about Wes over the past few weeks. "It feels strange knowing I won't see Wes until Monday."

Keaton squeezed her hand. "I'm sure he'll be fine."

"He seemed a little nervous."

"I bet he was. Applegate House is new, and he and his mom have been apart for a while. But, he's where he needs to be…with Claire."

Keaton was right, Tessa thought, as she watched him pull into a parking lot and maneuver his car into a spot near the restaurant's entrance. Wes was where he needed to be. He'd looked happy. Claire had looked ecstatic. And Tessa knew she should be feeling relieved and excited to have some time alone with Keaton.

So why did she feel so empty? "I know Wes and Claire need to be together, and that I've just been a glorified babysitter—"

"Tessa, we both know you've been more than that."

"I just feel like I'm at loose ends."

Sighing, Keaton said, "I guess I'm not going to have a choice, am I?"

Before Tessa could ask what he meant by that, he pulled her into his arms and kissed her senseless. Right there in the front seat of his Jeep, in the parking lot of Los Amigos, a Mexican restaurant she'd been really looking forward to trying out. At least, she'd been really looking forward to trying it until Keaton kissed her.

Now, all she wanted to do was snuggle closer and enjoy the sensation of his lips against hers, the sexy way he nibbled at her bottom lip, then explored her mouth with his tongue. Slowly, as if he had all the time in the world.

Finally, Keaton pulled back. "I'm going to kiss you like that every time you bring up that boy's name."

"Promise?"

He laughed. "Maybe not. But I will admit that I've been dying to have you all to myself. I've thought about tonight a lot."

Tessa knew what Keaton meant. He wasn't just talking about dinner and a few stolen kisses. He was talking about being *alone*, as in alone-with-no-clothes-on alone.

"I promise I won't say Wes's name for the next forty-eight hours," Tessa said, anticipating the moment dinner would be over and they'd be back inside her apartment.

Smacking his hand on the steering wheel, Keaton muttered, "Damn. You did it again." And true to his word, he pulled her close, kissing her again.

LOS AMIGOS HAD A VIBRANT atmosphere. Mexican flags, straw baskets, intricate iron sculptures and bright paintings decorated every inch of the restaurant. Loud music from a mariachi band and even louder chatter filled the room.

Tessa grinned. "What a great place! I can't believe I've never been here before."

"Want a margarita?"

"I think I'll just have a beer."

When the waiter stopped by, Keaton ordered two Coronas, which were quickly delivered to their table along with a basket of piping hot tortilla chips and salsa.

Keaton popped a couple of chips in his mouth. "These are terrific."

She bit down on one and nodded. They were good, but they could've tasted like cardboard for all it mattered. She couldn't seem to concentrate on anything other than the man sitting across from her.

"So, start talking," Tessa told Keaton.

"What?"

"I'm afraid to say anything," she said, only half teasing. If she started talking, she knew she'd be tempted to say a certain boy's name, just to feel Keaton's lips again.

He shook his head, obviously amused. "I love to hear you talk. You just have to remember your conversational choices."

"I'd rather play it safe and hear all about you."

A somewhat guarded look replaced his heated one. "There's not much to tell."

"Tell me more about growing up," she coaxed. "Where did you live? What sports did you play? As much as we've talked, you haven't told me much about your childhood."

"Well, let's see. I grew up in Fort Collins, Colorado. I have two sisters. In school I played football and wrestled. I went to Colorado State and met Susan. She wanted to move here to be near her family, so we did."

Tessa sipped her beer to keep from smiling at his brief life summary. "And you became a cop."

"It's what I always wanted to be." He shrugged. "I got married, I worked. She died, I worked some more."

"And now…"

A corner of his mouth lifted. "And now we're dating."

She liked the sound of that. "I'm glad."

"Me, too. What do you want to eat?"

She didn't care. "Whatever you're having."

"You're an easy date."

As she thought about how much she'd enjoyed kissing him—and how much she was looking forward to going back to their complex, she sighed. "You wouldn't believe how easy."

He grinned, signaled the waiter and ordered two combination plates.

Tessa told him about her parents and James, and he told her what it was like growing up with two sisters. She talked about working with Ryan and Jillian and about going to the apparel markets in Atlanta, Dallas and New York City, while Keaton filled her in on the daily workings of the police force.

Their plates came. Tessa supposed she ate, but she couldn't recall if she'd liked her meal enough to order it again. Keaton had another beer and pushed his plate aside, half-eaten.

"Tessa, this was great," Keaton said, as they waited for their bill. "Being with you…feels good. You've made me come alive again." He shook his head, a faint red hue spreading across his cheeks. "Sorry, I didn't mean to sound so corny. That really sounded over the top."

The thing was, it hadn't. His words had echoed the way she felt exactly. It was as if her world was the same but brighter, now that they had each other. "I know what you mean—I feel the same. I've looked forward to tonight like I haven't looked forward to anything in forever."

And because he still looked worried, tentative, and because she couldn't stop thinking about his kisses, she admitted one more thing. "And Keaton, I'm looking forward to later on, too."

"I…I've been with a few other women since Susan, but they weren't relationships. It's been a while."

"I know you've seen me on dates, but they weren't serious. I haven't had a serious relationship since college. So…it's been a while for me, too."

He blinked. "Since college?"

She nodded as she watched him mentally calculate. Saving him the trouble, she said, "Five years. Almost six." She tried to laugh it off. "I don't know how that happened." But she did. She didn't believe in casual sex. She'd wanted to wait for the right person.

But, like Keaton with his past, Tessa couldn't quite bring herself to share everything.

The waiter came with their bill. Keaton left a couple of twenties in the folder, then stood up and helped her with her coat.

Tessa followed him back out to the parking lot and they drove in silence through the dark streets until they arrived back at the apartment complex.

"Where do you want to go? Your place?" Keaton asked.

She didn't want anything to remind him of Susan. "My place sounds good."

He breathed deeply. "All right then."

Keaton stood to one side as she unlocked her door. Hung up her coat for her. Then, as Tessa stood in front of him, suddenly wondering if she should offer him a drink, he pulled her into his arms. Kissed her like he had in the Jeep.

"I want you, Tessa," he whispered.

Her whole body relaxed. It was happening. "I want you, too."

He nodded. Clasped her hand.

And guided her to her own bedroom.

Chapter Nineteen

Tessa's bedroom was pale pink. Fussy lace pillows, delicate china dolls and silly knickknacks adorned almost every surface. In the center stood a queen-size bed with layers of bedding piled on top. It looked inviting and cozy. Fresh…and utterly feminine.

As Keaton pulled Tessa into his arms, he caught her scent and realized with some surprise that her room smelled like her. He knew he'd just been allowed into a sanctuary few men had ever seen.

And he didn't want to be anywhere else.

Tenderly brushing her cheek with the pad of his thumb, he kissed Tessa deeply, savouring the taste of her, the way she pressed her body to his, making no attempt to hide her desire.

For a brief instant, their eyes met. "You okay?" he asked.

"I'm better than okay."

He pulled her closer and grazed her hips with his

own, letting her get acquainted with him, with what he wanted.

Softly laying sweet kisses along her delicate jaw, he ran his fingers through her soft waves of hair and plied all of her defenses with his tongue. Eagerly, she nipped at his upper lip. Smiled when he leaned down and unbuttoned the top button of her sweater. Gasped when he kissed the pulse points on her neck.

Oh, she was so sweet. She shifted restlessly, teetering on her heels. After steadying her, he bent down and gently removed each useless, oh-so-sexy pump.

And then, there was nothing to do but run his hands up her bare legs. He loved the fact that she favored skirts. Loved that she seemed to have no problem with him kneeling at her feet and getting up-close-and-personal with her legs.

When she parted her knees slightly, Keaton knew he was just about the luckiest man alive. And—being no fool—he decided to explore a little further.

With a gentle push, he guided Tessa down on top of her mountain of comforters. The feather cushions piled around her made her look as if she were lying on a cloud. Almost angelic.

Except she was looking at him in a way that was anything but innocent. Holding firmly on to his control, he perched on the edge of her bed, before bending down and pressing his lips to a silky patch of skin above her kneecap. Her breath hitched.

He nearly forgot to inhale.

Her soft, slim legs beckoned him and he pushed her skirt up even higher, swallowing hard when he spied the skimpiest pair of black panties he'd ever seen.

"Black satin, Tessa?" he asked teasingly, leaning on one elbow.

Her eyes popped open. Lifting her head to meet his gaze, she smiled. "Uh-huh."

He ran his fingers along the thin band of satin-covered elastic, enjoying how she groaned and fell back against her cushions again, letting him do what he wanted.

"You're full of surprises," he murmured, placing a kiss right under her ear.

With determined fingers, he unfastened another button on her sweater. Then a third. Gently pushed the soft material to one side. Maybe she had on a black satin bra, too?

Tessa squirmed, moving out of his reach before he got a good look at her. "You need to get undressed, too. This isn't fair."

"I think it's perfectly fair," he retorted. "Trust me, you are a much better eyeful."

"We'll see. Take off your clothes," she whispered, kneeling on the bed and helping him unbutton his shirt. She ran a hand across his chest, played with the patch of hair along his breast bone, then traced her fingers down his stomach until, at last, she reached the part of him that was begging to be noticed.

As she unzipped his pants and her fingers encircled him, he shuddered. With a dexterity he'd forgotten he possessed, he took Tessa's sweater off and unclasped her bra. His mouth went dry. It was all he could do to help her off with her skirt before tasting the smooth skin underneath.

Finally, when they lay together, skin to skin, his body begging for release, Keaton spoke. "It's...been a long time."

Tessa bit her lip. "I know."

He slid his hand down the length of her, amazed at her perfection, at how soft she was. "You're beautiful."

"You are, too."

Thankfully, he'd had the presence of mind to toss two condoms in his jeans' pocket. Keaton pulled one out and deftly covered himself.

He made love to her, as he'd been wanting to for weeks. Tessa rocked her hips against him, and he felt her nearing the edge. "Hold me close," she murmured.

"Always," he said, embracing her tightly.

Later, as he was drifting off to sleep, Keaton wondered just how long always was going to be this time.

Chapter Twenty

I want you, Tessa. Keaton's words still echoed in Tessa's head early Monday morning. So did the memory of his lips touching hers, the way he'd brushed his hands over her body. She felt tingly and alive. Fresh.

In love.

Tessa fingered the stack of fabric samples on Sylvia's desk, absently thinking how beautiful the finely woven material was, yet she had no real desire to fashion a garment out of it.

Suddenly, designing clothes—or even imagining a career with Designs for Success—couldn't hold her attention. All she wanted to do was think about her weekend. For three full nights she'd fallen asleep by his side. Each morning when she'd awoken, she'd felt his warm body next to hers, heard the comforting rhythm of his breathing.

It was as though a sixth sense would cause him to

open his eyes and smile softly. Within moments, she'd be wrapped in his arms, making love with him again.

This morning, they'd shared a quick cup of coffee before he'd run off to his shift. Then at eight, she'd picked up Wes and taken him through the McDonald's drive-thru on the way to school.

Tessa smiled as she recalled how Wes had opened up to her in the car.

"So, tell me everything you did yesterday," she'd said.

"First, Mom and I hung out and watched TV."

"What did you watch?"

"*The Price is Right.* Mom gets the Game Show Channel, too."

Tessa laughed. "Lucky you."

"Yeah." Picking up his Egg McMuffin, he added, "When Mom and me lived in the car, we never got to just hang out. We were always afraid."

"Why?" she'd asked, hoping it would do him some good to talk about his feelings.

"Mom was worried the cops would come and tell us to move. Or ask us where we lived." He'd looked down at the floor. "We used to go to a library so I could do my homework. One night the lady who worked there said people were complaining about us being there so long. We had to leave."

"Tough, huh?"

"Yeah. My mom started crying, but I acted like I didn't notice. It would've just made her feel worse."

Tessa had tightened her grip on the steering wheel, afraid to let Wes see how much his words were affecting her. "You were a big help to her. You still are."

"I guess. When we get our own apartment, I'm going to help Mom a lot. I told her I'm always going to make my own bed. And take out the trash."

"I'm sure she'll appreciate that." All she'd wanted to do was make him smile again. "I'm glad you and your mom had a good weekend. You said she liked to cook. What did you have?"

He'd wrinkled his nose. "Fish and green beans."

"What's wrong with that?"

"I hate green beans."

"How'd you like the fish?"

Brightening, Wes had told her, "We cooked the fish together. We rolled catfish in cornmeal and fried it up. Then, Mrs. Radcliff told my mom she bought all the stuff for ice-cream sundaes. I made one with three scoops of ice cream even though Mom said I only needed two."

"I would've done the same thing."

Wes had looked at her and giggled before taking another bite of his breakfast. "I know."

They'd continued to talk the whole way to his school, Tessa teasing him about his dislike of vegetables and Wes groaning and make gagging noises.

The drive had been fun. Comfortable. Special.

As Tessa ran her hands over the fabric, she knew her life was about to change.

When the time was right, Wes would move in with his mom, she and Keaton would need to discuss where their relationship was headed, and she would need to tell Sylvia that she was leaving S.Y.D. to run her own company.

She just had to figure out when the best time to do that would be....

"YOU'RE FIRED," Sylvia told Tessa that very afternoon.

"Excuse me?"

Sylvia rolled her eyes, as if she was talking to someone way below her intellectual level. "I've given this a lot of thought, and I'm afraid I have to let you go. You've hardly been around this past month."

"I've been around quite a bit. Enough to do more than my share of the work."

"While I appreciate your help, after much deliberation, I've decided to steer S.Y.D. in a new direction." Sylvia sat down behind her desk and motioned for Tessa to take a seat as well.

Tessa fell back into a plush chair, stunned. Sylvia's announcement made her feel as if she'd skipped a few pages in a book. What in the world had happened? The last she'd heard, Sylvia had been anxious for her to return full-time.

Once she'd had a chance to let it sink in, Tessa analyzed how she felt about being fired. And she realized it wasn't anger or upset that consumed her—it was relief.

Since her lunch with Mrs. Edwards, Tessa had given a lot of thought to Designs for Success. She'd gone on Google and researched everything she could find out about the program in other cities. In her heart, she knew it was something she wanted to do.

She just hadn't counted on it happening like this.

Sylvia pointed to the storage room. "We took the liberty of boxing your belongings. They're near the back door."

Without giving Sylvia another glance, Tessa marched out of the office. There, inside the storage room, sat a cardboard box with her coffee mugs and a couple of old sweaters inside. Right in the same place where she'd set her bag full of cans for Wes.

Next to her things stood Jillian, looking as if she was on the verge of tears. "Tessa, I'm so sorry," she sputtered. "Sylvia's been so awful and Ryan so confused, and part of me wants to quit, but I'm afraid to. I've got a possible upcoming wedding to worry about!"

Tessa reached out and hugged her friend. "Don't worry. It was time for me to go. This has just made it easier."

"Are you mad at me?"

"Never."

"Ryan and Sylvia had already boxed your things before I got here this morning."

"I'll finish up," Tessa said with a sigh, as she began to gather up the remainder of her personal items—her design books, her folders with contact information and her electric teapot.

It had been *her* idea, not Sylvia's, to start serving tea. Sylvia hadn't foreseen the benefit in pampering clients. Tessa had been the one to buy the tea and cookies. She'd also brought in the china service; it had been an old one of her parents'. No one had ever reimbursed her.

"That's my tea set."

Jillian nodded. "I'll help you pack it." She grabbed another cardboard box, neatly taped the bottom and began wrapping the delicate china cups and saucers in tissue paper.

Tessa scanned the rest of the storage room for her things. In the distance, she could hear the front door chime as customer after customer came in. The muffled sound of Sylvia's fake laughter floated through the walls. After a few minutes, Ryan showed up, looking debonair as always in a double-breasted suit.

He practically skidded to a stop when he reached for the teapot but only found a stack of tea bags. "Where's the teapot?"

Tessa pointed to her half-filled box. "In here."

"You can't take that. I need to make tea."

"Sure I can. It's mine."

"But it's been here for two years."

"And no one's ever reimbursed me. Sorry. *My* idea, *my* money, *mine* now forever," Tessa said, knowing she sounded completely childish but not caring.

Ryan cleared his throat. "Tessa, Mrs. Jackson is in the salon with a head cold."

Tessa paused in her wrapping. "And you're telling me this because…"

"You can't leave us in the lurch like this."

"Ryan!" Sylvia called out, impatience drawing out both syllables of his name. "I need you!"

Ryan turned to Tessa for help, his face slack with fear, and Tessa almost got up to help him—which was what she'd been doing since his first day on the job.

But then they both seemed to realize that things had changed.

Ryan raised a hand and waved goodbye. "I have to go," he said, a hint of regret in his voice.

Tessa mustered a smile for him, finished wrapping up her last cup, then hefted one of the boxes in her arms. There was no way she was going to exit through the alley like Sylvia would want her to.

Throwing open the door, she walked into the salon. "Tessa?" a cultured voice inquired.

"Hello, Mrs. Jackson," she said around the box.

"What are you doing?"

"I'm afraid I was fired today. I'm taking my things out to my car."

"Fired?" Mrs. Jackson turned to Sylvia. "Surely there must be some mistake."

"It's okay, ma'am," Tessa said, throwing a glance to Sylvia, who was standing by, seething. "A few weeks ago, I was asked by Mrs. Edwards to help start up a chapter of Designs for Success. I've been on the fence—now my decision has been made for me."

"Designs for Success? What's that?"

Tessa explained the mandate of the company, realizing how much she was looking forward to doing something meaningful with her life. "I've actually been helping a young mother get back on her feet, and she's agreed to be my first customer. I'm really excited about it."

"Well, I'd like to help out in any way I can," Mrs. Jackson said. "Give me a call, or have June Edwards do so." Stepping forward, she held out her arms. "Now, let me help you with your things."

Tessa handed her a lightweight tote bag. "Thanks for your help."

"My pleasure."

As they walked to the front door, Tessa glanced back toward Sylvia.

"Your name is mud," Sylvia announced.

Tessa's steps faltered. Not too long ago, Sylvia's statement would have chilled her to the bone. Now, Tessa heard it for what it was, an empty threat that had no bearing on her reputation.

"My contract states that I'm entitled to my final paycheck within two weeks of termination," Tessa said quietly. "I'll raise hell if you're late."

And with that, she stepped out into the bright Cincinnati sun, as S.Y.D.'s front door closed behind her for the last time.

Chapter Twenty-One

After the scene at Sylvia's, Tessa drove to Applegate House. More than ever, she was glad Mrs. Edwards had suggested Designs for Success. She was also glad that she and Claire Grant had become friends. She was looking forward to talking with her, testing out some of her ideas on her. She was going to need all the help and advice she could get.

Once she arrived at the shelter, one of the women informed her that Claire was at work, so Tessa drove to the hospital. Rather than taking the highway, she took a shortcut through some residential neighborhoods. As she passed a row of bungalows, she had to smile. Almost every house was already festooned with twinkling lights, Christmas trees illuminating two or three windows. Here she was, trying desperately to keep some order in her life while the rest of the world had started decorating for the holidays. Some of them probably already had a turkey in their freezer.

Thanksgiving was now just over three weeks away. She loved the holiday and everything it stood for. And this year, more than ever, she was looking forward to seeing her parents and enjoying their peaceful company.

After asking around, she found Claire mopping floors near the labor and delivery area.

Claire glanced up as Tessa approached. "Is everything okay? Is something wrong with Wes?"

"Everything's great," Tessa replied, thinking how happy she was that Sylvia had just made her life easier. "I got Wes to school this morning just fine. Do you have a few minutes to talk?"

Claire glanced at the clock at the end of the hall. "I get a fifteen minute coffee break every two hours. I can take it as soon as I finish mopping this section."

Tessa took a seat in a nearby grouping of chairs, content to watch Claire while she waited.

The difference in Wes's mom was incredible. There was absolutely no sign of the frail, sickly woman she'd been when Tessa had first met her. With easy motions, she ran the mop over the floor. When an elderly couple stopped and asked for directions, Claire guided them down the hall with confidence. The month of forced rest, medicine and counseling had worked wonders.

After rolling the mop and bucket back into a supply closet, Claire carefully stepped across the damp floor. "Would you like a cup of coffee?" Tessa asked her.

"No, thanks. I've already had a few cups today." She sat down in the chair next to Tessa.

"How's everything going at the shelter?"

"Good. Mrs. Radcliff, the director, has her hands full, dealing with all of us. We're a pretty interesting group of women. Lots of personalities, to say the least."

"Have you met anyone you think you'll be friends with?"

"Yes, a couple of people." Claire paused, smiling into a ray of sunlight streaming through the window. "Actually, I've been on my own so much, I kind of forgot how to cultivate friendships. It's going to take a while. But, having Wes stay over on the weekend was nice. He did okay. *We* did okay." She squeezed her hands together.

Tessa felt her eyes prick with moisture. Claire's strength was awe-inspiring. "How's your job?"

"Fine. I'm grateful for the work." A shadow crossed her face. "I don't know if I can ever convey what it was like to always live in fear."

Tessa chose her words with care. "Wes mentioned it was difficult."

"And scary. I was always afraid someone was going to find out how we were living." She shook her head. "When I got sick, I thought nothing could be any worse. Now I'm realizing that nothing could have been better for our future."

"So, what's the next step?"

"Well, I talked to Wes this weekend, and we both

feel that it's time he moved to Applegate. A few of the women there have offered to help watch him while I'm working. We thought next Saturday might be a good time for him to start."

Tessa swallowed as a sharp, sudden sense of loss hit her. She was going to miss Wes. "Sure, but don't forget, you can always call me if you need someone to watch him."

The look Claire gave her was full of understanding. "I won't forget." She narrowed her eyes, then, and frowned. "How are you doing? Are you okay?"

"I honestly don't know if I am or not." Tessa chuckled. "I was fired today."

"What?"

As briefly as she could, Tessa filled Claire in on everything that had happened in the past week, including her decision to open a Cincinnati branch of Designs for Success.

"Wow."

"Wow is right. Like you, I'm beginning to think that my worst fear—losing my job and my references—might have been one of the best things to happen to me. I'm really excited about starting this new career."

Claire reached out and clasped Tessa's hand. "You should be. It's going to do a whole lot of people a lot of good."

Tessa hoped so. She squeezed Claire's hand, so grateful for her friendship. "My mother always says that everything happens for a reason. I think she may be right."

Claire smiled.

"My break's almost up—was there anything else you wanted to talk about?"

"Actually, I need to ask you a favor."

Claire leaned forward, her eyes revealing her eagerness to pay Tessa back in any way she could. "Name it."

"Would you be my first client?"

"Don't you think you've done enough for me?"

"You've helped me, too, Claire. Please don't think our relationship has been one-sided. You've helped me learn more about myself—more about who I am and who I want to be. If we hadn't met, I don't think I would've ever had the courage to switch jobs."

Casting a glance down the hall, Claire patted Tessa's hand. "We can talk next Saturday when you drop Wes off."

"I'll plan on it."

Claire stood up. "I've got to get back to work."

"Okay. Wes and I will stop by tonight to visit. And Claire?" Tessa added, reaching out and touching the woman's arm.

"Yeah?"

"Thanks."

Claire's face lit up and she gave her the warmest of smiles. "Thanks, to you, too."

Chapter Twenty-Two

Keaton woke to brilliant sunlight filtering through his curtains. Wearily, he lay back down and did his best to cover his eyes with his pillow.

But the darkness didn't do much except bring back the last twenty-four hours in vivid color. Yesterday, he and Genevieve, along with two other teams, had spent too much time at an accident off I71. A teenager had died, and with his death had come all of the forensics specialists and photographers who appeared when a tragedy occurred.

Such a waste. He'd notified the parents. Their horror and dismay at losing their son would be forever implanted in his mind.

Even Genevieve, who never cried, had looked dangerously close to breaking her own rule.

Of course, the accident wasn't the only reason he hadn't slept well. His mind had kept flashing back to last evening. Tessa had shared her news about being fired with him, and at first she'd tried to act as if it was amusing, but before he knew it, she'd been crying in his arms.

With time, her tears slowed and his consoling kisses had turned into passionate explorations. They'd broken apart, both very aware of Wes in the back bedroom. He'd left soon after, taken a cold shower and gone straight to bed, sure that the day's events would guide him into a deep sleep. But instead he'd dreamed.

Of Susan.

Sweat beaded his brow as he recalled the images. She'd been laughing, her long brown hair swinging past her shoulders. She'd looked beautiful. Happy. He'd felt a surge of happiness, too.

They'd been sitting at her favorite café, and she'd been sharing stories about her day, running errands. Susan could make going to the grocery store seem like an adventure. He'd held her hand and felt so at peace.

Peaceful in a way he hadn't felt in a long time.

Sighing, he sat up, knowing it would do him no good to lie in bed and think about how much he missed his wife. Just like it didn't do him any good to feel guilty every time he realized a whole day had passed that he hadn't grieved for her.

But as he sat there in bed, all he could think about was Tessa—and all he felt was the same sense of tranquility he'd drawn from his dream.

The realization shocked him. In response, he

quickly turned to Susan's picture, but found yet another surprise. At some point, her photo had fallen in between his bedside table and his bed. As he reached for it, he noticed that the silver frame bore a light coating of dust, proof that it had lain abandoned for some time without his knowing.

Keaton held the frame on his lap, smiled at Susan's pretty black-and-white photo, and wondered if this was a sign for him. "Did you do this on purpose, Sue? Did you come into my dreams just so I could remember you...and say goodbye?"

His voice echoed in the room, but an even stronger feeling of peace filled him. Sometime between the night Tessa had come to him looking for help and now, he'd begun to live again. "I think I'm going to put your picture in the living room, Sue. I miss you. You know that. But...it's time for me to be thankful for what I have."

And with that, he carefully carried her framed picture and set it on the end table next to his sofa. Then, he padded over to his kitchen phone and called Tessa.

"What are you doing, calling this time of day? I thought you'd be at work," Tessa said, her voice tensing. "Is something wrong?"

"I'm actually still at home," he said, curling his toes into the nap of the living room carpet. "I'm working second shift today, so I slept in. What are you doing now?"

"Not much."

"Are you hungry? Do you want to go to the diner with me in about fifteen minutes?"

"Why, that's the best offer I've had all morning," she said brightly. "I'd love to."

TESSA COULDN'T HELP BUT notice that, wherever they went, Keaton was the kind of guy who attracted attention. His rugged handsomeness and his quiet, powerful demeanor caused more than one woman at the diner to sneak a second glance in his direction.

But he seemed content to ignore them all. In fact, today he seemed a little withdrawn. Once they'd eaten a good portion of their pancakes and were sipping their coffee, Tessa decided to ask him about it. "Is something wrong?" she asked, pointing to the way he'd been absently circling his mug around and around in his hands. "You're going to rub the logo off the side if you keep that up."

Startled, Keaton glanced down, and stopped the nervous movement. "Sorry."

"Is it a case you're working on?"

"No." He pressed his lips together. "I found Susan's picture on the floor this morning."

She didn't know what to say to that. But, supremely aware that the find was important to him, she asked, "Is it okay? Did the glass break?"

"It's fine." He sighed. "Tessa, I realized that it had been there for a while and I hadn't even noticed. I always used to look at her photo before I went to sleep…I can't believe I didn't notice sooner."

Panic set in. Panic that no matter how close they'd gotten, Keaton's heart was still miles away. Panic that he was looking to her for support and that she was going to say the wrong thing. "You've been busy…" she offered lamely.

"There's more. I dreamed about her last night. She was…the same. So beautiful. So upbeat."

Tessa took a fortifying sip from her now lukewarm coffee. There was no way she could ever compete with Susan, or her memory. Not that she even wanted to, but she'd hoped that one day there would be room in Keaton's heart for her, too.

"I would've been happy to be married to Susan my whole life," he continued. "She was a great wife, a great partner." Quietly, he added, "She would have made a good mother."

"I'm sorry," Tessa said, knowing her condolence was woefully lacking. Keaton's burdens were heavy, and the fact that he felt he could share them with her was a big step forward.

Still, she couldn't help feeling selfishly depressed. She'd spent the last few days thinking about him, dreaming about being a real parent with Keaton by her side. "I'm so sorry," she repeated, her voice cracking. "I know she was a very special woman."

He nodded. "She was. She gave me a lot of comfort."

"I'm sure she loved you, too, Keaton." Tessa

breathed deep as a sinking feeling settled deep within her. She realized she was completely in love with Keaton and he was about to break up with her. Biting her lip to keep it from trembling, she sat stoically and waited for him to tell her what was on his mind.

He shook his head. "I know she loved me. But, that's not what I wanted to talk about. Tessa, I realized that while I'll always hold Susan close to my heart…she's part of my past. I miss her, but not with the ache that I used to feel."

Tessa could hardly breathe for the hope that bloomed inside her. "And?"

"And I feel like her picture falling was a sign that it's okay with Susan if I move on." He bit his lip. "I guess you must think I'm crazy, believing that a dead—"

Tessa pressed two fingers to his lips, stilling his words. Her emotions were running amok. "I'm glad Susan's letting you know everything's going to be okay."

"I put her picture in the living room," he said, holding her gaze with his eyes. "For some time—I don't know how long—I've only been thinking about you." He gently skimmed his thumb across her cheek. "Tessa, I've fallen in love with you."

She blinked. "I…"

"You don't have to say a word," he murmured. "I just wanted you to know that my feelings for you are real."

"I love you, too," she said quickly, surprised at

how easy the words were to say. Surprised at how they filled her up inside, as if she didn't need anything else. His love, and her love for him, was enough. "I love you so very much." *As much as Susan did,* her heart promised.

"I never thought this would happen again," he admitted.

"I never thought I'd fall in love at all."

As their words hung in the air, a clatter of dishes in the background reminded them that they were far from alone.

"Tessa." The longing in Keaton's voice sent heat coursing through her veins.

All she wanted was to be in his arms again. "Do you think we could leave?"

"Yeah. I'd like to take you into my bed."

Making love with him, feeling his warmth, enjoying his touch...nothing sounded better. "That sounds perfect."

He pulled out a crumpled twenty from his pocket. "Let's go."

Chapter Twenty-Three

"I don't know why I thought I could do everything so quickly," Tessa said with a groan. "Setting up this business is taking about twenty times longer than I thought it would."

As Jillian glanced around Tessa's new, very cluttered office, she shook her head. "I don't think you're giving yourself enough credit. Things are coming together." Pointing to Tessa's computer, which was up and running, and the neatly organized bookcase, she stated, "You've already accomplished a ton."

Tessa surveyed the room with fresh eyes. Maybe Jillian was right. In the past week and a half, she'd leased her space, bought most of her supplies and had phone lines installed. Mrs. Edwards's clout in the community had helped rush things along.

"I guess things are in pretty good shape. If I could convince another five people to donate clothing or services today, I'd go to sleep happy."

Jillian carried a box of gently used handbags into Tessa's garment room and gestured for Tessa to follow. "Hey, here's an idea." She began unpacking the bags and lining them up on a metal shelf. "Go to sleep happy no matter what. Your life is pretty terrific."

Tessa thought about her new business venture and her relationship with Keaton. More importantly, she recalled yesterday's phone call with Wes. He and his mom were doing just fine, cooking and watching game shows together.

"You're right. I have every reason to be happy."

As they continued to work on sorting the donations, she asked, "What are you and Todd doing for Thanksgiving?"

"Nothing, really. My parents are flying to Detroit to see my sister and her family. Todd's parents already have plans serving dinner at a shelter downtown." Shrugging, Jillian said, "I guess Todd, Bill and I will be enjoying our first Thanksgiving alone."

Tessa chuckled. "You, Todd and *Bill*. That puppy has taken over your life."

"Only a part of it," Jillian protested. "I can't help it—he's so cute."

"I think a quiet holiday sounds romantic."

"Maybe," Jillian held up a tweed blazer for inspection. "I'd rather be looking forward to a big gathering. I'm one of those people who actually likes to be around friends and family on holidays."

"Maybe one day you, Todd, Keaton and I can plan to celebrate a holiday together."

"What about you and Keaton?" Jillian asked. "Is he going to go to Columbus with you?"

"I asked him, but he has to work the next day, so he said it might be difficult. He'll probably go to the station on Thanksgiving. Volunteers bring in dinners for the officers on duty."

"How are things between you two?"

"Great." Better than that, Tessa reflected. Now that Wes was staying with Claire, she and Keaton were developing a new routine. After a simple dinner, they'd watch TV and talk about their days. Keaton had begun to open up more about his day-to-day work on the force. She was happy that she could be a source of support for him, just as he'd been such a huge source of support with Wes.

Opening another box of clothing, Tessa said, "Thanks for helping me today, Jillian."

"My pleasure."

"I hope that even though we won't be working at Sylvia's together, we'll still be close."

"Of course." With a big grin, Jillian added, "After all, I'd never forgive my maid of honor if she disappeared from my life."

"Maid of honor? Really?"

"Yup!" Flashing a beautiful diamond solitaire framed in a band of gold, Jillian teased, "You must be preoccupied. I've been waiting for you to notice my ring from the moment I walked in here."

Tears sprang to Tessa's eyes. Jillian's hand looked so right sporting that diamond. "It's gorgeous," she said. "Perfect for you."

Jillian beamed. "The wedding's going to be in May. Will you please stand up with me? I can't imagine getting married without you there by my side."

Tessa reached out to hug her friend. "You know I'd be honored."

"Good. Now, since you're going to be in the wedding, any chance you'll consider designing the gowns?"

Tessa grinned. "No problem. I've already got something in mind."

"I HOPE YOU HAVEN'T BEEN waiting too long," Claire said, hurrying into the Designs for Success office. "I was able to work a couple of extra hours at the hospital, and I couldn't turn it down."

"You couldn't, or didn't want to?" Tessa asked, already knowing the truth.

"Didn't want to," Claire admitted sheepishly. "I've been wanting to do everything I can so they won't regret hiring me."

"Claire, from the things you've said, it sounds like they've been really happy with you. Didn't your supervisor suggest you apply for the opening in radiology?"

"She did." Her eyes shining, Claire exclaimed, "Oh, Tessa, it would be so great. It's a receptionist position—I'd be greeting patients and doing clerical work—but there's room for growth. If I took classes, I could be a technician...do ultrasounds or even MRIs." She shook her head. "I filled out the paperwork, but I don't know if they'll ask me for an interview."

Tessa had been in contact with the hospital earlier and had found out some good news, but she wanted to keep it a secret a bit longer. "Come in and have a seat. Tell me about you and Wes."

"Things are going really great," Claire said, sitting down in a chair across from Tessa's.

"How does Wes like the shelter? He hasn't said too much about it in our phone conversations."

"I think he likes it fine. There's another woman who recently moved in—she's got a daughter named Jyl. Wes and Jyl have kind of hit it off."

Tessa leaned back. "I imagine it's nice to be around other kids who've been through some tough times, too."

"That's what Mrs. Radcliff said. She said that counseling would help, or at least spending some time talking about what we've been through. The sessions have been good for Wes. I'm finding out that he coped with everything by saying he was fine." Pursing her lips, Claire added, "I believed him. Now that he's starting to open up, I'm realizing he wasn't fine at all."

Seeing the concern in Claire's expression, Tessa patted her hand. "This may be overstepping my bounds, but I got the feeling that he really *was* fine in a lot of the ways that counted. He had you…"

"And all of my problems." She rolled her eyes. "I'm sorry. I told myself I was going to concentrate on the future, not the past."

Squeezing Claire's hand, Tessa said, "Let's go ahead and get started. First, I'd like you to take a peek at some clothes in the other room. I have a feeling you're going to want to look your best for your upcoming interview."

Claire froze. "What?"

"I'm sorry for not telling you right away, but I wanted to surprise you. The director of the radiology department scheduled an interview for you on Saturday morning."

Claire's smile faltered as her control crumbled. "I didn't expect anything to happen so soon."

"When I called the hospital administration office this morning, I spoke with Jim Mathers, the director. After chatting for a few minutes, I told him about my business and how one day I'd love to help you prepare for an interview, whenever the time was right. That's when he cut me off. He said the staff has been pleased with your work and attitude, and that they think you might be a great fit for that receptionist position."

A tentative light entered Claire's eyes. "Wouldn't that be something?"

"I think it's going to happen." Tessa bit her lip. "So, will you still let me help you prepare for your big day?"

Claire nodded, smiling eagerly, and followed Tessa into the garment room. "Wow," she said, looking around at all the racks of business suits, shoes and handbags.

Tessa grinned. "Let's see. You must be about a size six. Look around and see if anything catches your eye."

Cautiously, Claire approached the clothes, looking at each outfit but not touching anything. "They're all very pretty."

Tessa was surprised at the woman's reticence. She'd expected Claire to jump right in and select a few items to try on. "How about this one?" Tessa asked helpfully, holding up a periwinkle number. "The color suits your complexion, and it would brighten up those cloudy days."

Holding it in front of her, Claire said, "It *is* nice."

Hearing the hesitation in her voice, Tessa gestured to the rack again. "Or maybe you'd be more comfortable in a sweater set and slacks. I guess it might be overkill to wear a suit to your interview." She plucked a soft ivory cardigan off its hanger. "This would look good on you."

As if prodded, Claire tried the sweater on over her shirt and studied herself in the mirror.

When Tessa became aware that Claire was trying hard not to cry, she grabbed her hand. "What's wrong? Did I say something?"

At S.Y.D., she was used to her customers being assertive and expecting the same type of service. But then, those women were quite different from Claire. Perhaps she found all the attention embarrassing. "If you'd like me to leave while you look, I can—"

"No, it's all right," Claire said, her voice heavy with emotion. "It's just that this whole experience is pretty overwhelming. I mean, Tessa…a month ago I was living in my van. I was so sick I didn't know how I was going to get better. I had my son helping me collect cans for gas money!" She sighed deeply. "Now I've got a job interview, a place to stay, Wes is flourishing…and I've got you."

"Me?"

Claire laughed through her tears. "Yes, you, Tessa. What if you'd never helped Wes and me? Where would we be without you?"

They stared at each other for a moment, each silently conveying a wealth of emotions. They really had come a long way.

They both had a lot to be thankful for.

With a shake of her head, Claire reached over and retrieved the periwinkle suit. "I'd like to try this on. I don't care if it's a little too dressy. I've earned the right to look terrific!"

"That's more like it!" Tessa said. She reached for one of her client forms and attached it to a clipboard. "Okay. As soon as you decide what you want to wear, we'll make an appointment for the makeup and hair people to come in."

"What are you talking about?"

"Oh, honey, you're going to get a complete makeover."

Claire's mouth dropped open in shock. "I haven't done any of that in a long time…ever, actually."

"It's about time then, don't you think?"

New tears formed in Claire's eyes. "I don't know what to say."

"Don't say anything."

Claire gave her a look.

"Okay, then, how about this—one day, when you meet a gal at the hospital who's down on her luck, be her friend. Share your story. Tell her about Applegate. Tell her about Designs for Success. I don't want this to be a one-shot deal."

Claire smiled. "Okay. I accept. Now what?"

"I'm going to hand you a list of questions. Take them home, think about the answers, then come back tomorrow and we'll play job interview."

"You're going to coach me?"

Tessa nodded. "You're going to be fine. I promise."

Chapter Twenty-Four

Claire did come back the next day and the day after that. Tessa went over different interview techniques with her, such as looking people in the eye and using life experiences to illustrate her qualifications.

With each meeting, Tessa felt surer of herself, and of her decision to start the business. Already, Janet Hughes had arranged for her to meet with two more women, and Keaton had recommended her to a third.

Mrs. Edwards had also been busy, calling everyone she knew. Two of her socialite friends had offered to volunteer ten hours a week to help Tessa get Designs for Success off the ground.

Early on Saturday morning, Tessa went to Applegate and helped Claire get ready for the interview. Then, Janet came by and picked up Claire so Tessa could stay with Wes. As they watched Janet's sedan pull away from the curb, both she and Wes breathed a sigh of relief.

"So, here we are again." Tessa was pleased to see him smiling. "Want to go to Pluto's Pizza for lunch?"

He tilted his head in the way Tessa knew so well. "Maybe."

"*Maybe?* Are you joking?"

Flashing a grin, Wes repeated, "Maybe." He shrugged on a jacket and waited for her to button her coat. "Mom looked really pretty."

"I think she did, too."

They walked to her car. Wes climbed in his side and turned to her after they'd both buckled in. As if reading her mind, he whispered to her, "I think we're going to be okay now, Tessa."

With those words, Tessa knew it was true: things *were* going to be okay…and different. Wes and Claire were already talking about moving into an apartment. "I *know* you're going to be okay," she said with certainty.

As she turned the corner and they both chuckled at an inflatable green Grinch bobbing on someone's front lawn, Wes said, "Think we'll still see each other? You know, after my mom gets her job and we move?"

Her breath hitched. What would she do if they drifted apart? Not wanting to seem too pushy, she said as casually as she could, "I sure hope so."

They sat in silence for a few minutes, Tessa's mind spinning from all of their recent changes and adventures.

"So, when we get there, want to order a pepperoni pizza?"

Unable to stop herself from laughing, Tessa nodded. "Of course we'll get pepperoni pizza. I know you don't eat any other kind. A whole pitcher of pop, too. After all, we've got a lot to celebrate."

"I got an A on my science test."

"Shoot, we might even have to go out for ice cream, too. That stuff about the food chain was hard. I didn't think we were ever going to master it."

Wes's eyes shone. "I'm glad we met, Tessa."

Impulsively, she reached for his hand and clasped it tight, remembering how she'd once been too afraid to hug him. "Me, too, honey. Me, too."

THE MORNING BEFORE Thanksgiving dawned bright and beautiful, a marked contrast from the last two days, when the snow squalls and freezing temperatures had pretty much shut the city down.

The only consolation for most people was that Dayton and Columbus had been hit worse, though that wasn't much of a comfort to Tessa. For the first time in her life, she wasn't going to be with her family on the holiday. Highway conditions between Cincinnati and Columbus were bad enough that warnings were posted hourly to stay off the roads if at all possible.

After the craziness of the past few weeks, Tessa was bitterly disappointed. She'd been looking forward to sipping hot tea with her mom and sharing all her stories of the past month and a half with her family. Slumping down on her couch, she gazed at the frost-covered window. "Well, at least now we'll get to be together tomorrow," she told Keaton.

"You don't need to sound so excited."

"I'm sorry. It's just that Thanksgiving has always been a time for me to get together with my family."

"Let's start a new tradition." Picking up the phone, he said, "I'm going to invite a few other people to come over."

"Okay," she said hesitantly. "But you know I don't cook."

"You worry about decorating. No one's asking you to cook."

Hope bubbled up inside her. "You think we'll be able to get a good crowd together?"

"Positive. We're not the only people snowed in."

"TESSA, IT'S ONLY 8 A.M." Keaton said Thanksgiving morning. "Come back to bed."

She glanced at him. He looked warm, virile and absolutely at home among all her pillows. "I can't. I'm too keyed up. Besides, Claire and Wes should be here in two hours. Wes is going to watch the parade with me."

"It's good they're coming over early. Claire's got to get that monster turkey you bought in the oven."

"I wouldn't call it a monster—it's only twenty-four pounds."

"It's gargantuan."

"I like big birds."

"Obviously."

His voice, so tempting, almost made her want to crawl back into bed with him. "Um, what time did Gen say she was coming?"

"Noon. Gray's coming, too."

"Do you think something's up with the two of them?"

"No way. Genevieve's like one of the guys."

"Just because you think so doesn't mean Gray does."

"I know Gray. Genevieve's terrific, but there's nothing going on between them. Gen's been hinting that she might leave CPD. I think she's applied for a position in one of the suburbs north of here."

"Because of us?"

"I don't think it's the only reason. I think she wants a change—to go somewhere with closer ties to the community. She may be tough, but she's a small-town girl at heart."

Thinking about how a major life change had been so right for her, Tessa nodded. "I hope she finds what she's looking for."

Fluffing up a pillow and placing it behind him, Keaton sat up, the covers settling over his bare hips. "Come here for a moment. I want to talk to you before everyone comes over."

Finally giving in, she hopped up on the bed and curled next to him. "What about?"

"You. Me. Thanksgiving."

Alarm bells went off in her head. "Did we forget something? Cranberry sauce? *Had she forgotten cranberry sauce?*

"Stop." Tenderly, he took her hand. "Have I told you lately that I'm truly thankful for you?"

She swallowed. Shook her head.

"I am. I'm thankful for the way you've turned my life around. How you've brought light into it again. I'm thankful for the way you've reminded me that tomorrow is something to look forward to. I want to plan a whole future together."

Her heart practically stopped beating, his words meant so much. Kissing him, she whispered, "I'm thankful for you, too. You've helped me remember things about myself that I'd forgotten. You've given me the confidence to dream about a bright future. I'm a better person because of you."

"So…will you marry me, Tessa?"

She looked in his eyes, and they shone right back at her. Green, reflective, honest. His love for Susan, deep and true, was evident…as was his love for her. "You sure?"

He groaned. "Only *you* would ask that. Tessa, I'm trying to—"

She spoke quickly. "Yes. Yes!"

His arms tensed around her middle. "Good."

He looked so smug and satisfied, she couldn't

help but tease him. "Good? What kind of answer is that? You're supposed to—"

He pulled her closer and covered her mouth with his. "Is this okay?" he asked when he drew back.

Their bare skin touching did feel awfully good. "Yes."

He raised one eyebrow. "Anything else I'm supposed to do? I mean, I want to do this proposal thing right."

"All you have to do is say you love me."

"I love you. I'll love you forever," he whispered, punctuating each word with a kiss. He raised his head. "Better?"

Since she was already melting, she could only nod.

His hands—those hands she loved—caressed her back. "I know *exactly* what to do next," he said.

Tangling her legs with his, she had no doubt he knew exactly what to do. "Claire and Wes..." she murmured.

"We have over an hour."

"Salad—"

"Shh."

His hands glided across her shoulders and pulled her even closer.

"Keaton?"

He didn't even try to look patient. "Not another word, Tessa."

For once, she was only too happy to comply.

Chapter Twenty-Five

"I didn't think Bill could jump that high," Jillian moaned to Todd as she wiped the puppy's nose. "I guess he really likes candied yams."

As Bill yipped in protest, Todd picked up the casserole dish and eyed it skeptically. "There's a big indentation on the left side where the dog got into it. Any thoughts on what you want to do with the rest, Tessa?"

"Throw it out. We love Bill, but I don't think anyone wants to eat his leftovers."

"I don't. I hate yams," Wes announced.

Claire took the dish from Todd. "Maybe there's a way to salvage it," she said patiently. "I don't think Bill touched anything over on this side."

"Maybe he did, Mom. Maybe he slobbered all over it."

Claire shook her head in exasperation. "I don't think so."

Handing the squirming puppy to Wes, Jillian said, "Wes, would you go play with him? Todd and I are going to help your mom in the kitchen."

"I could do something," Tessa offered.

All three adults shook their heads. "We've got it under control," Claire said.

Knowing she was of no use to them, Tessa wandered into the living room where Genevieve and Gray were sitting on the couch, watching the football game and discussing each play. "Sorry things are so crazy."

"Not a problem. It feels like home," Gen said.

"It wouldn't be Thanksgiving without something going wrong," Gray added.

Keaton stepped behind her and rubbed her shoulders. "Stop worrying. Everything's fine." Leaning closer, he whispered, "Look around you, Tessa."

Gen and Gray had returned to yelling at the TV as if the coaches could hear them. Wes was sitting on the floor in the dining room playing with Bill. Claire, who now was a receptionist at the hospital, was carefully doling a portion of the yams into a plastic container. Jillian was placing the rolls in a basket, her diamond engagement ring glinting in the bright light coming through the window. Todd was sneaking a piece of turkey.

It looked like a family.

Tessa knew those friendships were her greatest gifts. She was thankful for each and every person there, and the difference they'd all made in her life.

"Can we eat now?" Wes asked, walking over to Tessa, Bill following in his wake. "I'm starving."

"Only if you say grace."

"No problem. That one's easy," he said, leading the way to the table. "All you have to do on Thanksgiving is say what you're thankful for."

Keaton rubbed his head. "And what are you thankful for, sport?"

"Everything," Wes said solemnly. "I'm thankful for everything."

Tessa squeezed his hand. "Me, too, Wes. I'm thankful for everything, too."

* * * * *

Experience entertaining women's fiction about rediscovery and reconnection—warm, compelling stories that are relevant for every woman who has wondered "What's next?" in their lives. After all, there's the life you planned. And there's what comes next.

Turn the page for a sneak preview of a new book from Harlequin NEXT.

CONFESSIONS OF A NOT-SO-DEAD LIBIDO
by Peggy Webb

On sale November 2006, wherever books are sold.

My husband could see beauty in a mud puddle. Literally. "Look at that, Louise," he'd say after a heavy spring rain. "Have you ever seen so many amazing colors in mud?"

I'd look and see nothing except brown, but he'd pick up a stick and swirl the mud till the colors of the earth emerged, and all of a sudden I'd see the world through his eyes—extraordinary instead of mundane.

Roy was my mirror to life. Four years ago when he died, it cracked wide open, and I've been living a smashed-up, sleepwalking life ever since.

If he were here on this balmy August night, I'd be sailing with him instead of baking cheese straws in preparation for Tuesday-night quilting club with Patsy. I'd be striving for sex appeal in Bermuda shorts and bare-toed sandals instead of opting for comfort in walking shoes and a twill skirt with enough elastic around the waist to make allowances for two helpings of lemon-cream pie.

Not that I mind Patsy. Just the opposite. I love her. She's the only person besides Roy who creates wonder wherever she goes. (She creates mayhem, too, but we won't get into that.) She's my mirror now, as well as my compass.

Of course, I have my daughter, Diana, but I refuse to be the kind of mother who defines herself through her children. Besides, she has her own life now, a husband and a baby on the way.

I slide the last cheese straws into the oven and then go into my office and open my e-mail.

From: "Miss Sass" <patsyleslie@hotmail.com>
To: "The Lady" <louisejernigan@yahoo.com>
Sent: Tuesday, August 15, 6:00 PM
Subject: Dangerous Tonight
Hey Lady,
I'm feeling dangerous tonight. Hot to trot, if you know what I mean. Or can you even remember?☺ Look out, bridge club, here I come. I'm liable to end up dancing on the tables instead of bidding three spades. Whose turn is it to drive, anyhow? Mine or thine?
XOXOX
Patsy
P.S. Lord, how did we end up in a club with no men?

This e-mail is typical "Patsy." She's the only

person I know who makes me laugh all the time. I guess that's why I e-mail her about ten times a day. She lives right next door, but e-mail satisfies my urge to be instantly and constantly in touch with her without having to interrupt the flow of my life. Sometimes we even save the good stuff for e-mail.

From: "The Lady" <louisejernigan@yahoo.com>
To: "Miss Sass" <patsyleslie@hotmail.com>
Sent: Tuesday, August 15, 6:10 PM
Subject: Re: Dangerous Tonight
So, what else is new, Miss Sass? You're always dangerous. If you had a weapon, you'd be lethal.☺
Hugs,
Louise
P.S. What's this about men? I thought you said your libido was dead?

I press send, then wait. Her reply is almost instantaneous.

From: "Miss Sass" <patsyleslie@hotmail.com>
To: "The Lady" <louisejernigan@yahoo.com>
Sent: Tuesday, August 15, 6:12 PM
Subject: Re: Dangerous Tonight
Ha! If I had a *brain* I'd be lethal.
And I said my libido was in hibernation, not DEAD!
Jeez, Louise!!!!!
P

Patsy loves to have the last word, so I shut off my computer.

* * * * *

Want to find out what happens to their friendship when Patsy and Louise both find the perfect man?

Don't miss
CONFESSIONS OF A NOT-SO-DEAD LIBIDO
by Peggy Webb,
coming to Harlequin NEXT
in November 2006.

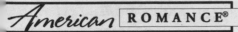

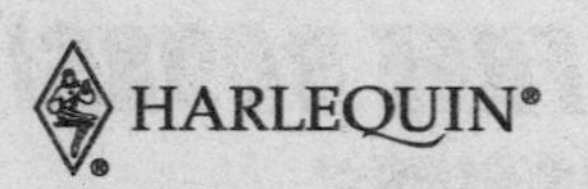

COMING NEXT MONTH

#1137 THE CHRISTMAS TWINS by Tina Leonard
The Tulips Saloon
When Zach Forrester first meets Jessie Farnsworth she's in need of rescuing—and an attitude adjustment. After a passionate encounter, reason sets in and Zach realizes Jessie may be pregnant with his child. But can Zach's determination and Southern charm convince Jessie to let him into her heart in time for the holidays?

#1138 LONE STAR SANTA by Heather MacAllister
A false money-laundering charge sends Mitch Donner back to Mom and Dad's for the holidays. Kristen Zaleski is about to make it big in Hollywood—until an empty bank account lands her back in Sugar Land, Texas. Both sets of parents agree—it will take a Christmas miracle to get their kids out of the house. But is this too big a job, even for Santa?

#1139 THE QUIET CHILD by Debra Salonen
Sisters of the Silver Dollar
When her ex-fiancé asks Alex Radonovic to help his son, her first reaction is to refuse. After all, the child is proof of Mark's betrayal. But her heart goes out to the sad little boy, and she recalls her mother's prediction. *A child's laughter can heal a wounded heart, but first you have to heal the child.* By helping Braden, will she finally be able to forgive his father?

#1140 COURT ME, COWBOY by Barbara White Daille
Baby To Be
Miller men were unlucky in marriage. Or so Gabe thought until his ex, Melissa, came back to him in time for Christmas and gave him the most precious gift in the world. She was determined not to stay, but he was just as determined to change her mind—*before* she disappeared with his son....

www.eHarlequin.com